PASS INTERFERENCE

EMILY SILVER

TRAVELIN' HOOSIER BOOKS

Flag on the Play

Pass Interference:

Definition: A judgment call made by an official who sees a defensive player make contact with the intended receiver before the ball arrives, thus restricting his opportunity to catch the forward pass.

Chapter One

COLIN

"Want a blow job?"

I swirl my drink as the lights strobe around me. The blonde sitting next to me had my number the minute I walked into this club tonight. I can't say that I mind the attention. Being in my position, it comes easily.

"Sure."

The dark corner of the club hides us as she slides my zipper down and takes my dick into her warm, wet mouth. Alcohol swirls through my veins as I lose myself in this woman. Shit, what was her name again? I can't even remember. Not like I'll remember it after tonight anyway.

The feel of her lips wrapped around me brings me closer to the edge. She sucks and licks her way down my dick. It's easy to get lost in her. To turn off the noise in my head.

A tiny voice in the back of my head tells me I shouldn't be doing this. But as the mystery woman—Carli maybe?—swirls her tongue around the head of my dick, I'm exploding down her throat.

"Fuck." I close my eyes, resting my head on the back of

the seat. I will myself to feel better about this than I actually do.

This has been my scene for as long as I've been in the league. But right now, I can't muster up any energy to care for the person beside me. It makes me the worst kind of dick, but I couldn't care less.

The blonde in question tucks my now limp cock back into my pants, wiping her mouth as she straddles me.

"Care to go back to my place?" Her lips are wet and her eyes hazy. A switch flips, and the last thing I want to do is head back to her place.

I stand, setting her on the padded seat of the booth.

"Sorry, babe, gotta go."

"What, that's it?" Her voice is high and shrieky. It tells me I'm making the right choice here. Jersey chasers are all the same—wanting to get in the sack with a football player. They don't care who, just as long as they get one.

I drop a kiss on her cheek. "Practice in the morning. Don't worry, I'll cover your tab."

She sneers at me. "You're a dick."

"Never said I wasn't."

I leave my tab open for her at the bar and head out into the humid Denver night. It's pushing one a.m. Tomorrow is going to be a bitch.

It's one of the first optional off-season training days before camp starts in two weeks.

The team says it's optional, but it looks bad if you aren't there. And with the madness of football season starting soon, I knew I needed to blow off some steam tonight.

I know I'm a dick, but jersey chasers are perfect for a quick release.

No emotion, no attachment. It's how I've been living since joining the Denver Mountain Lions. Might not be the most meaningful of existences, but it's easy and works for me. Because it allows my sole focus to be on football.

And not anything else that I'm missing in life. Or the who I've been missing in my life all these years.

THE BLARING ring of my phone pulls me from sleep. I know that ringtone. I set it specifically so I could ignore it. Sunlight beams in through the open curtains in my room. The buzz from last night has worn off.

Blessedly, the ringing stops. But the buzzing doesn't. I groan, rolling over to grab my phone off the nightstand. Hundreds of notifications light up my screen.

Fuck.

This time, when my dad calls again, I answer.

"What the actual fuck, Colin?"

I wince, pulling the phone away from my ear. "What is going on?"

His scorn is felt through the phone even from hundreds of miles away. "Have you not looked at the news today?"

"Christ." I scrub a hand down my face, not wanting to actually do it.

"It's almost eight. Get out of bed and call me when you do."

He ends the call. The last thing I'll be doing is calling him back. When I notice a missed call from my agent, I know shit's hit the fan.

I call him back without bothering to open any notifications on my phone.

"Colin. Seems you've really stepped in it this time." Earl doesn't beat around the bush, getting straight to the point. It's one of the reasons he's my agent.

"What's going on?"

"Looks like the woman you were with last night did not appreciate how you treated her. There's an article circulating about what a 'pompous, egotistical man-whore' you are." He clears his throat. "Her words."

"Fuuuuck."

"I've already had three calls from Denver's management this morning. This doesn't look good, Colin."

"You think?" I snap. Now I'm on edge. Sure, it might've felt good last night, but now I'm paying the price.

"You're in a contract year. Players have been traded for a lot less. You know this isn't how Denver likes their players to act."

"It's not like they know everything."

Earl guffaws. "Yes, I will be sure to tell them that this one woman isn't even the tip of the iceberg. I'm sure they'd love to know how many women you've actually been with."

"What can I do?" I ignore him, trying to go into problem-solving mode. I know Earl has cleaned up a few messes for me here and there, but most of the time, I keep my business to myself.

"Maybe think with your brain next time."

I roll my eyes. Climbing out of bed, I find discarded sweats on the floor and pull them on. My footsteps echo throughout my empty house as I head toward the kitchen. It's too early to deal with this conversation and not have caffeine in me.

"So what, is this like my third strike and I'm gone? No longer a Mountain Lion?" Even as I say the words, I feel the crack in my chest.

Denver is all I've ever known. I went straight from Knoxville to Denver and haven't looked back. To think I could lose everything because of one mistake makes me sick to my stomach. I've never claimed to be the smartest guy in the room, but I never thought what I was doing would jeopardize my spot with the team.

"Tell me I didn't fuck up too bad, Earl." Maybe if I say it, I can will it to be true.

"I have a meeting with the GM today. You go to practice and act like everything is fine."

"And then what?"

I start the coffee that's waiting to be brewed. I could use a shot of something stronger right now, but it's probably not the best time.

"Then you go home and stay at home. I don't want to see your ugly mug on any newspaper or tabloid for the rest of the season. There's no room for you to fuck up again. You hear me?"

His tone is final.

I suck in a lungful of air, trying to take in what his words mean for my future. I nod, knowing full well he can't see me.

"Do you understand me? I don't think I need to impress upon you the seriousness of your situation."

"I understand. Boy scout from here on out."

"Good. Stay by your phone. I'll call you once I know more."

He ends the call without another word.

What the fuck did I do to myself?

Chapter Two

PEYTON

"How about this outfit? Does this one work?" I turn, checking the skirt from all angles in the mirror.

"It looks fine," Grier replies.

I aim a glare her way in the mirror. She's nestled among piles of clothes on my bed. "It can't be *just fine*. It has to be perfect if I want to nail this job interview."

Grier twirls a lock of auburn hair around her finger. "You'll nail it based on the fact that you're you."

"That's not a vote of confidence."

"They'd be crazy not to take you on. You're one of the smartest people I've ever met."

I slip out of my skirt and toss it onto the bed. I've known Grier since my first day of grad school. If it wasn't for her, I don't think I would have made it this far into the program. CU Boulder has one of the hardest sports management programs in the country. It was a lot of late nights studying and then passing the time between tests with margaritas and occasional shots of tequila. But lots of margaritas.

"If I get this internship, who knows how many doors it could open for me? I need to be better than fine. I need to be sharp."

"Don't get yourself worked up. It'll only stress you out more." Grier stands, swatting my ass as she goes to my closet. Shifting through what little remains, she pulls out a sleek black dress. "Wear this. Pair it with my snakeskin heels and your necklace and you'll look like a badass."

I toy with the necklace, tracing its worn letters. Even after all these years, I've never been able to take it off. It's my safety net, even though that person is no longer in my life.

"You're right. Simple and classic."

"Damn straight. You're too in your head about it. You're going to crush this interview. They'd be stupid not to take you."

I steel my spine, taking her words to heart. "You're right. I'm going to be the best damn intern they've ever seen. And when I graduate, I'll have my choice of jobs."

"That's the spirit." Grier claps me on the shoulder. "Now, how about some shots to calm you down?"

"Grier!" I shriek. She cackles as she makes her way into the kitchen. Changing into sweats and a T-shirt, I follow her. "There will be no drinking tonight. I need to be fresh and clear for tomorrow."

"Relax, girl. You've totally got this. You know more about football than anyone I know."

I fidget with my necklace. It's a nervous habit. "But what if there's a better candidate out there?"

I want this position so bad, I can taste it. Everything I've ever wanted is right in front of me. I grew up surrounded by football. With a dad who was the team doctor for the Tennessee college football team, it was hard not to love it.

And now that I have a choice, I want to work with any team that will have me.

Except Vegas. Never Vegas. Biggest bunch of cheating assholes I've ever seen.

"Do we need to go review how kickass you are again?"

I grab a soda from the fridge and crack it open. "I'm allowed to be nervous. This is only my future we're talking about."

Grier ignores me. "You crushed the GRE. You have the highest GPA of anyone in our program, me included." She ticks each item off her fingers as she goes. "The fact that you even have an interview with Markham and Associates is unheard of, plus you have the opportunity to join them even before the semester starts. Do you know how hard it is to get in with them?"

I nod my head. I've been the envy of everyone in our class. "But it's only an interview."

"But with Earl Markham, an interview is as good as getting the job."

This time, I can't help the smile that spreads across my face. "Stop getting my hopes up."

"Hopefully you'll get to work with the hot players."

I swat at her hand as she starts taking out leftover cartons of Chinese food. "I'll be lucky to work with any players right now. If I get the job, I'll be on scut duty. Coffee runs for weeks before they even know my name. I'll be 'hey you' to most people there."

Grier laughs, but I know the minute she thinks what I've been thinking. "He doesn't work with Earl, right?"

I cringe. "No. The last time I checked, he was with a company based in Vegas."

Grier shakes her head. "Thank God for that. Can you imagine having to see your ex every day?"

"How about that shot?" Anything to get her to stop talking about my ex.

She claps her hands. "Finally! Just one. For good luck!"

"I'll need all the luck I can get."

"SO TELL ME, Peyton, why is it that you want this position?" Tammy, the older woman I've been interviewing with, is tough but fair. She's made it easy to settle in to this interview. I've been able to answer all of her questions without turning into a bumbling idiot. Something about being around powerful women always puts me at ease. It's like I can see myself in their shoes and want to mirror their every move.

"I grew up around football. I've always loved sports, and it's the one thing I've always wanted to do with my life. Social Media Management is something a lot of teams aren't great at. Teams like Denver have a great social media footprint, but others—like Vegas—don't. I want to learn from the best so I can be an asset to whichever company I go to work for."

"And what would you say if we sent you to work with one of our hockey stars?" She gives a playful smile.

"I've been following Colorado's team since I moved out here, so I'd be happy to do it. They were just on the brink of getting to the playoffs this past season."

Tammy tucks a gray strand of hair behind her ear. "I'll admit, you know your stuff. Most women that come in here can tell you the stats of everyone we represent, but not so much the teams. I'm impressed."

"Like I said, I grew up around sports. I love all of them."

"Even golf?" Tammy laughs.

I smile. "Even golf. Just don't ask me to play."

"No, none of that. You'll likely be a floater. Earl might have you work on some special projects of his as well. We'll need you to be adaptable."

Her words have my ears perking up. Discussing what I might be doing has to be a good sign. "I can be adaptable."

"We don't believe in having you go on coffee runs." Tammy smiles. "Although that might happen on occasion, Earl makes it a point to give his interns a well-rounded experience. If you're going to be working at Markham and Associates, he wants you getting the real deal."

"That sounds great."

"With this being your last year of school, have you thought about what you want to do after you graduate?"

"Yes!" I say with a little too much enthusiasm. "I mean, yes. I'd love to be able to stay in Denver. Maybe get a job here. Or work with one of the teams in the city."

"I'm glad you're already thinking about it. I think you'll do great here, Peyton. We're excited to have you join the team." Tammy stands.

"So I have the job?"

She nods, a smile plastered on her face. "You do. We'll have you start Monday. Some basic paperwork, company policies about no fraternization and kickbacks, things like that. Nothing too grueling. We'll let you get the lay of the land before we throw you off the deep end."

"I'm ready for it." It's hard to contain my excitement. "Thank you, Tammy."

Tammy extends her hand and I take it, probably shaking it with a little too much vigor.

I follow her through the cubicles, imagining myself

being a part of this team. It's one step closer to my ulti-mate goal.

"We'll see you Monday," Tammy says, waving me out.

"I can't wait to get started."

Chapter Three

COLIN

"There's our pompous, egotistical man-whore," Knox shouts from the other side of the locker room. What feels like every set of eyes zeroes in on me as I walk across the spacious room to my cubby. Even the Mountain Lion logo on the floor seems to be judging me.

"I'm surprised you know those words. They're pretty big for you," I deflect, flipping him off.

"I told him to keep his trap shut," Jackson mumbles beside me as he pulls on his knee brace. "Trust me, being in the media for that reason isn't fun."

I know Jackson went through some shit last year with his ex. At least this was a problem of my own making.

"How bad is it?" Alex asks, pulling his practice jersey over his head.

"Eh. Just need to keep my head down and not get into any more trouble. It'll be fine." I try to play it off like it isn't a big deal.

Maybe if I keep telling myself that, I'll start to believe it.

"Colin! See me after practice!" Coach Brooks shouts from his office.

"Fine, huh?" Jackson asks. "You sure about that?"

"Fuck."

If Coach wants to talk to me, I'm guessing it's worse than I thought. My phone buzzes from where I set it down in my locker. Seeing it's my dad again, I ignore the call.

"Not another woman in your little black book?" Logan pipes up from the other side of Jackson.

"Worse. My dad."

"Not pleased with seeing his son in the tabloids?" Knox asks.

"More like telling me how I'm screwing up both of our lives at the same time."

"Damn, he sounds like a dick," Logan says.

I nod my head. "You're telling me. Took me a long time to realize that."

After each game, my dad would dissect every single thing I did wrong. No matter if I had a touchdown or broke the team's passing record, I could have done better. It should've made me hate the game, but it only gave me the determination to be the best damn wide receiver out there.

I wanted to do it to spite him.

The money I earn each year is a big fuck you to him. Even on a rookie contract.

"Think you can make it through practice without landing in the spotlight?" Knox claps me on the shoulder.

"I don't know. Is your mom out there? Maybe I can go home with her."

"Fuck you." Knox flips me off.

"Aww, you don't want me to be your new stepdad?" I say, shoving him as we head out to the practice fields.

"Don't think I won't tackle you to the field the first chance I get."

"He deserves it at this point," Jackson says, tugging on his helmet and heading off in the opposite direction from us.

"Young! James! Quit the chitchat and get over here!" Our offensive coordinator calls us over.

"What's the game plan for today?" Alex asks.

Going over what we're working on, I shift my focus to running plays. This is where I'm most comfortable. I know these plays like the back of my hand.

Getting lost in practice is easy. The feel of the grass beneath my cleats, the perfect spiral landing in my hands —all of this is easy.

It's the other noise that gets me in trouble.

We run drill after drill. Our coordinator drew up some new plays that we're practicing together. Working them through with Alex is always fun. After getting drafted at the same time, we know where the other will be before we even think it.

It makes these new plays easier to grasp.

And before I know it, practice is over.

Ignoring everyone in the locker room, I head straight for Coach's office. Better to go ahead and get this over with.

I knock once before I'm beckoned inside.

"Have a seat, son." Coach motions to the chair in front of his desk. "I'm assuming you know why you're in here?"

It'd be stupid to play dumb at this point, so I give him a straight answer. "I do."

His stare has me squirming in my seat. Coach is not someone to mess with. He's a man of few words. Someone you would do anything to win for. He's one of the best coaches I've ever had, and the gaze he's giving me isn't something I'm used to.

"Colin, do you like being on this team?"

My response is quick. "More than anything."

"Then why would you do something so stupid that could jeopardize your position here?"

I clear my throat, drier than sandpaper. "I guess I didn't think—"

"That's the problem. You didn't think," Coach cuts me off.

I wipe my hands on my pants, my palms sweating with nerves.

"Whether you realize it or not, you're in a position of power. You can use that for good, or you can do things like you did the other night."

I wince, thinking of Coach seeing the articles. I'm sure he did, as did everyone in team management.

"Am I being cut?" The words blurt out of me before I have a chance to even think more about it.

"Right now? No."

I heave a sigh of relief.

"But don't take that to get complacent about your place on the team. The GM informed me you'll have a meeting this afternoon with your agent. They've worked out a plan to help you get back in the good graces of the team and our fans."

"And if I do well at that?"

"Then we shouldn't have any other problems." His tone is final, dismissing me. But he pulls me back.

"One more thing, Colin."

"Yeah, Coach?"

"I don't think I need to impress upon you the importance of sticking to the plan. One wrong move and you could be gone. And I really don't want to have to trade you. You're the best wide receiver we've ever had, and I'd hate to think this could be a difference maker for you staying or going."

"Whatever it takes, Coach."

He nods and I leave.

My skin feels two sizes too small as I head back to my locker. Knox looks like he's ready to say something, but whatever he reads on my face stops him. Stripping out of my practice clothes, I grab a towel and hit the showers.

Resting my hands on the tile, I let the hot water wash over me. It eases the stinging of muscles after a hard practice.

The best part about football is leaving everything out there on the field. Whatever I'm feeling, I put it into practice or a game.

God. Why do I have to think with my dick so much?

It's been like this ever since I got drafted. I didn't want to have to focus on what I lost, so it was just easier to lose myself in women that didn't mean anything.

Maybe this is the wake-up call I needed. To get my shit together and finally move on with my life.

It happened five years ago. I should be over it. I can put the past behind me and move on.

Except moving on still makes my heart squeeze in my chest. At least the damn thing is still in there. And maybe I'll force it to move on.

Once and for all.

Chapter Four

"How's the first day treating you?" Tammy pops her head over the cubicle wall.

I give her a shy smile. "Feeling a little overwhelmed. But I'm excited."

I've worked hard for this position, and no matter what they throw at me, I'll give it everything I've got. Because succeeding here is as good as gold in the industry.

"Well, if you're ready, Earl wants to see you. He has a project that I think you'll enjoy."

"Absolutely!" I shoot out of my chair. I'm way too eager, but I don't care. I want to do a good job here.

Working for an NFL team has been my dream for as long as I can remember. With one more year of school left, it's finally within reach. It's so close, I can almost taste it.

I follow Tammy to Earl's office and take a seat. Even though Earl runs the show, Tammy is the one who is going to be following my progress throughout the internship. She's nice, but no-nonsense. It only adds to the pressure to do a good job.

"Peyton. Are you ready for your first big assignment?"

"Yes." I infuse more confidence in my tone than I'm feeling. Earl has a big presence. He's one of the top agents in the sporting world. He represents a list of the who's who of the sports world. Doesn't matter the sport, everyone wants him. And I want to impress him.

"We have a bit of a situation with one of my newer clients. He's been around the league for a few years, but let's just say, he has an image problem." Earl steeples his hands in front of him, almost as if he's assessing me.

"What can I do to help?" I shift in my seat, ready to get started.

"We're going to need to work on a rehabilitation plan for his image. Show the public he's more than just some playboy."

Ideas start whirring through my head as to what I can do.

"This is a contract year for him," Earl continues. "He loves Denver and doesn't want to leave."

"I can understand that," I tell him.

Colorado has been my home away from home the last few years. Aside from having one of the best grad programs for the concentration I wanted, I love being surrounded by the mountains. It reminds me of home. Whenever things got to be too much, I could head to the mountains and all would be right with the world.

"We need to drum up some good press for him. And that's where you will come in. Plan outings for him that will remind the city why they love him. Keep him in line. That sort of thing."

"I can do that."

Earl aims a beaming smile in my direction. "I have no doubt. Tammy will be monitoring your progress throughout the semester, but if you need any help from either of us, don't hesitate to ask."

"You can count on me." I sit straighter.

"Colin should be in shortly, and we'll go over everything with him and introduce the two of you. But I'd like a preliminary plan to Tammy by the end of the week. With the season starting, time will be more limited, so you'll need to get creative."

"Colin? As in Colin James?" My throat is like sandpaper. The memory of his face slams into me. The easy smile that always brought out his dimples. The way his brown hair was always falling into his face. And his eyes. Lord, could I get lost in them.

"The one and only. Have you followed his career?" Earl glances up at me over a stack of papers. I do my best to school my expression.

"He went to Tennessee, so I followed him there. But not since he entered the league."

"That's right! How could I forget those Volunteer connections? Did you two know each other?"

I give Earl my best fake smile. Because of course my first big assignment would be with the man who broke my heart in college. "We were both there at the same time and had a few classes together."

"That should bode well then. I'll let you get started, then I'll bring you in once Colin and I have a chance to discuss this new plan."

"He doesn't know about it?" I can't hide the trepidation in my tone. If there's one thing I remember about Colin, it's that he hated being bombarded with anything he didn't know about. Which sucks for him being in a profession where you can be traded on a whim for any reason.

"That's for me to worry about. Now, go off and come up with brilliant plans."

More like coming up with a plan to get through these next few weeks as fast as possible.

Because having to work with the guy who walked away from me is going to be the hardest thing I've ever had to do.

Colin

"YOU'RE serious with this shit, Earl?"

"If you didn't sleep with everyone in Colorado, we wouldn't be having this discussion right now."

Earl pins me with a fierce look. He became my agent last summer after my old one retired. I like Earl. Most days he's fair and will work to get me the best deals out there. But not today.

"What all do I have to do?" I lean forward, elbows on my knees. This day has been never-ending.

"Cut this playboy shit, Colin. You're better than this. But until you can prove that to me, the Mountain Lions management, and the fans, I'm bringing in some help."

"What kind of help?" A sick feeling settles in my gut.

"Someone to keep you on the straight and narrow. I know how much playing for the Mountain Lions means to you, so shape up or they'll cut you faster than you can say free agent."

I scrub a hand down my face. If I had a penny for every time I've heard that today, I could retire now. "It's not like I'm hurting anybody."

"I'm sure that woman who gave the tell-all would disagree."

"Fucking jersey chasers," I mumble.

If looks could kill, I'd be six feet under. "Denver has a

reputation around the league. They don't put up with hotshot players or those that don't represent their values. You're walking a fine line, James."

"You sound like my dad."

"Do you listen to him?"

"No." The only thing he cares about is football, and fuck if I'm going to listen to a word he says.

"Then listen to me. Because otherwise, I'll be shopping you around next season. Unless you want to end up in Vegas, I'd start looking less player and more team player."

I grimace. The last thing I want is to leave Denver. I was drafted here when I came out of college and this place has become home. "Then what do I need to do?"

"Ahh. Here she is now." Earl stands, turning his attention away from me.

Following his lead, I stand and turn to face the newcomer in the room.

Except it's not a newcomer at all.

No.

It's someone I'm intimately familiar with.

The woman who stole my heart freshman year and never gave it back.

"Colin. This is Peyton, our newest intern. Peyton, this is Colin. You might recognize each other from UT. You two will get to know each other very well these next few weeks." Earl claps me on the shoulder as I try to keep the confusion at bay.

"I'll leave you two to get to know each other, and then Tammy will be along to go over the plans we have for you."

"Sure thing, Earl." I don't look at him. My gaze is fixed solely on the woman in front of me.

Fuck. She's even more gorgeous than she was in college. Long brown hair curling down her chest. A skirt-

and-blouse combo that clings to her gorgeous curves. Deep brown eyes that give nothing away.

That's new. I used to be able to read her like a book. But now? Nothing.

I shouldn't be looking at her like this, but I'm in shock.

The smack of papers on the desk brings me back to the present.

"I'm sure Earl has told you why we'll be working together." Her gaze is fixed on the desk.

"What the hell are you doing here, Rocky?" The old nickname slips out.

Peyton's fiery eyes snap up to meet mine. There's the girl I used to know.

"It's not like I'm stalking you, if that's your concern." She crosses her arms in front of her chest. "And you can call me Peyton."

A thousand thoughts are swimming through my head.

The last time I saw Peyton, I was dropping her off at her dorm, telling her I'd see her after our business midterm. I kissed her goodbye and that was it.

I never saw her again.

"You didn't answer my question. What are you doing here?"

Peyton pins me with a focused stare. "Not that it matters to you, but I'm finishing my master's degree this coming year. And this internship is the last step of the process."

"So what you're saying is, you need me?"

"God, this is never going to work." Peyton slaps a hand over her eyes. "Were you always this much of a dick in college?"

"Hmm, funny. I seem to recall you being a fan of my dick back in college."

Peyton removes her hand. The icy glare she sends my

way sends shivers down my spine. "No wonder you're in this mess in the first place. All you can think about now is your dick."

"Why are we still talking about my dick?" I quirk a brow in her direction.

"You're right. No more dick talk." Peyton gives me a sickly sweet smile, taking the seat across from me and folding her arms over the pile of papers on the desk between us.

"What do you want to talk about then?" The last thing I want is to be sitting in a room with Peyton, but it will alert Earl if I storm out of here. I'm already in hot water; no point in making it worse.

"I've been working all afternoon on coming up with a plan to make the Denver fans fall back in love with you. With my help, it should be pretty straightforward."

"So what, you're like my babysitter now?" This morning, I was doing my best to not think about the woman who broke my heart. Now she's sitting in front of me, in control of my own destiny.

"For lack of a better word, yes."

"Jesus," I mumble.

"Don't think I'm excited about it either. But Earl seems to think we'll work well together."

"Does he know about our past?" I whisper. Earl's office is small, but gossip tends to run rampant around these places.

"Are you crazy? I spent almost an hour listening to the no-fraternization policy this morning. Earl would lose his mind if he knew," Peyton hisses.

Her automatic anger toward me sends my hackles rising.

"At least he'd know why I am the way that I am," I mutter under my breath.

When you lose the girl of your dreams, you do whatever it takes to numb the pain. And that's exactly what I did.

Numbed the pain any way I could.

Namely, women.

But apparently I wasn't as quiet as I thought because Peyton slides the folder my way. There's a flash of something across her face, but before I can pin it down, it's gone.

"Tammy had me comb through all your past tabloid exploits to get a handle on what I'd be dealing with. To say it was an enjoyable experience would be an overstatement." She looks down at her hands, clearly not wanting to see these images again.

Jesus. Every article ever printed about me is in here. Some are better than others, but none are great. No wonder I'm in the hot seat.

"What did you come up with?" I close the folder, not needing to see anything more.

"A goodwill campaign. If people don't like you off the field, they won't cheer for you on it. Denver isn't Vegas. They care how their players act off the field."

I nod. "Okay."

"I've started with a few events. The Mountain Lions Women's group—"

"Is that really a good idea?" I cut her off.

"Have you ever been to one of their events? They do a lot of good work for the Denver community at large, so they'd be a good group to win over."

"Okay."

She quirks a brow at me before continuing. "There's also a Labrador retriever rescue that will be hosting an adoption day. They'll be a great partner for you. Ongoing support and such."

"Okay."

Peyton ignores me. "There'll be a charity auction for dates with players. Not the best event for you, but Earl says you're committed, so that one has to stay." She shuffles her stack of papers around.

"Okay."

"Stop saying okay!" She gives a frustrated groan.

"What else can I say? Seems to me like if you say jump, and I don't say how high, I'm done."

"Are you going to be like this the whole time?"

"How am I?"

"Disagreeable and combative."

"And how should I be? Seems like you know everything."

"Can you not be civil? It will be easier for both of us."

"Fine. Just tell me when and where I need to be, and I'll do it."

"That and football. That's it." She points a finger at me.

"Got it."

"Good."

"Great."

The tension in the room is not something I'm used to with this woman. She literally holds my entire future in her hands. One wrong move, and she could go running to Earl.

And to think, Peyton used to be my everything. We had plans. I was going to play in the NFL, and she was going to make a name for herself in the league doing whatever amazing things she could do.

But then she left.

We somehow failed each other.

Now, if I fail her, I fail the team.

And that's one thing I can't afford to lose.

Chapter Five

PEYTON

"**A**re you shitting me?" Grier gasps, covering her mouth with her hand. "Colin freakin' James is your pet project for this year?"

I nod, gulping down the rest of my wine. "How do I manage to land my dream job with the one guy on the planet that I can't stand?"

Grier shakes her head. "You have the worst luck."

"God, and I have to help him rehab his image. Do you know what a slut he is?"

"Do I really want to know?"

I cringe. "No. Some of the things I saw I can never unsee."

"Was he like this in college?" Grier holds the wine bottle out to me, but I shake my head.

"Not even before I met him. I have no idea who this Colin is."

"How are you going to handle seeing him every day?"

"I don't even know. I never thought I'd see him again, and now I'm going to have to see him every day. Every day. Do you know how many days there are in a week?"

Grier gives me a *duh* look. "Honey, you're spiraling."

"You would be too if you had to work with your ex!"

"Can you remember any of the good times you had?" Grier asks with an innocent expression on her face.

I finger the necklace that I could never quite bring myself to get rid of. Colin and I had nothing but good times in college. There was the occasional fight, but we were hot and heavy from the minute we first got together.

"It's hard to reconcile the person he was with the person he is now. I don't even recognize him."

"Maybe that'll make it easier to keep things professional."

"I hope so. The last thing I need is him screwing up this opportunity for me."

"Can you picture him with no clothes on? Isn't that what people always say?" Grier asks.

I burst out laughing. "I think that's for speaking in public."

"Maybe he could take a lesson."

"In keeping his dick in his pants?"

Grier nearly chokes on the sip she just took. "Shit, Peyton. Warn a girl next time." She wipes up the wine that spilled down her chin.

"It's his dick that got me in this mess."

"Why are we still talking about his dick?"

"You're the one that brought it up."

"I believe you did," Grier corrects.

I roll my eyes, pouring myself another glass of wine. "Seriously, Grier. What am I going to do?"

Now the panic starts to set in.

Everything I've ever wanted is within reach. Long before Colin ever entered my life, my dream was to work with an NFL team. It's so close, I can taste it.

And now, the one man I was happy to never see again is standing between me and that goal.

I need to keep my heart locked away tight. If I can make it through this semester, I know I can pretty much do anything.

"I'm just going to keep my nose down and not get sucked back into Colin's bubble."

"And maybe don't look at his dick."

Chapter Six

COLIN

"Can you really not keep it in your pants?" Knox asks, pumping the weight bar.

"Do we have to talk about this?" I wipe the sweat from my brow.

"Dude. You were all over the news because you got a blowjob and left the girl," Jackson pipes up from where he's doing sit-ups. "That's a dick move."

"I never said it was my finest moment, you fucker." I throw my towel in his direction. "I just…I don't know. I got caught up in my head."

"Could you maybe get caught up somewhere else? Maybe without your dick in someone's mouth?" Alex is resting his forearms on the weight bar that Knox abandoned. We spend more time in here, it seems, than anywhere else in the building.

"I don't think I've ever heard so many guys talking about your dick before." Logan laughs.

"Better his than mine," Alex states matter-of-factly.

"Fuck you, guys. This is serious. What happens if I get cut?"

Logan's face goes pale. "You're shitting me."

"Denver won't actually cut you, will they?" Jackson whispers. Almost as if saying it out loud might make it come true.

"Fuck if I know. But I don't think Earl would say it if it wasn't a possibility. I'll be a free agent next year."

"So you put your entire career at risk for a mediocre blowjob." Alex shakes his head. The disappointment coming off him is palpable. "You're supposed to be a captain."

Alex's words couldn't cut deeper if he tried.

"Fuck."

I know I screwed up, but having to deal with Peyton now on top of everything else?

"How are you going to fix this?" Jackson asks. "Now that I'm back this season, we have a real shot…"

He doesn't need to tell any of us what we have a shot at. Football players are a superstitious bunch.

"Earl has this grand plan to make me lovable in Denver fans' eyes again."

Knox snorts. "Then you're well and truly fucked."

"Dude, not helpful," Jackson chirps.

"What's Earl's plan?" Alex asks.

"A complete rehaul of my image," I grumble.

"Oh, this is too good." Knox laughs.

I scrub a hand down my face. "I'm glad my misery is so amusing to you."

"Look, Earl wouldn't steer you wrong." Alex and I have the same agent, so I know he sees it the same way I do.

"It's just that I have to contend with this person who is in charge of the plan who might make my life miserable." I don't let on who she is.

"Oh fuck. Do I even want to know?" Knox asks.

"Maybe a little humility would do you some good."

Alex eyes Knox. The two of them exchange a skeptical look.

"Hey, I can be a humble person, you fuckers."

"And you're actually going to try? I mean, make this plan work so you don't get cut?" Jackson asks, his tone weary. "God, I feel sorry for this person."

"I'm sure she'll do just fine."

"Oh God, it's a woman? Now I really feel sorry for her," Jackson jests.

"Not all of us have only ever dated two people." I flip him the bird. "Besides, I can keep it in my pants if it means the team is better for it."

"Should we make a bet on this? I feel like this would be easy money," Knox asks the other guys.

"Hey!" I try to defend myself. "If this ever happens to you, just know I'll be rooting against you."

"No way. You like all of us too much," Logan says with a hopeful look in his eyes.

"You're all a bunch of assholes." I go back to my weights.

"But a lovable bunch of assholes." Logan gives me a smile that I'm sure he's used on a jersey chaser or two.

"Still assholes."

"Coming from this asshole, can you at least keep your shit together to make it through the season?"

I give Alex my smile that I know charms everyone. "When have I ever not had my shit together for the season?"

Alex rolls his eyes. "I take back what I said. You're fucked, man. Well and truly fucked."

"ANOTHER ROUND? LAST CALL."

Sometime in the last hour, the bar emptied around me. After everything that went down today, I needed to get out of my head. Did I mean to ignore everything Earl told me *not* to do?

No.

But I was going stir-crazy in my house. It felt like the walls were closing in on me, and I needed a breather.

"Another beer, thanks." I tip my glass in the bartender's direction.

The thing I like about this place? They don't ask a lot of questions. I can sit here in my own misery. I've never been one to mope, but after an ass chewing from Earl and the team?

Yeah, I want to mope.

A beer is set in front of me, and I drink down the icy liquid. It does a lot to settle my frayed nerves.

Thank God for this small hole-in-the-wall near my house where I can get some peace and quiet.

Well, mostly quiet. Until a familiar sound comes from behind me.

"What part of stay home did you not understand?" The anger dripping from her words has me spinning on my barstool.

I don't think I've ever seen Peyton so angry. Or more beautiful. In a simple white T-shirt and leggings, no makeup, and her hair in a complicated-looking bun, she reminds me of the girl from college.

Which pisses me off even more.

"What the fuck are you doing here?" I turn back to my beer, dragging a finger down the icy glass.

"Earl called me. It's now my job to keep you in line."

"How exciting for you." My voice is flat.

"Yes. Just how I wanted to be spending a Thursday evening. Coming to some bar to drag you back home."

"Careful. People might think you like me."

A sardonic laugh bubbles out of her. "Oh yes. Let me throw myself at you like every other woman in Denver. How'd you know I couldn't resist you?"

The sarcasm in her tone cuts deep.

"Fuck this. I had to get out of my house. No one said you needed to come get me."

Peyton holds up a finger as she opens her phone. Swiping, she shows me a Twitter notification from an hour ago.

MtnLionsFan87: Colin James looks to be spending the evening alone at a local watering hole. Act fast ladies!

A PICTURE of me sitting alone at the bar is under the tweet.

Fuck. Me.

"It's not like I asked for someone to take that picture."

Peyton shakes her head. "It doesn't matter. You're a sports star. You're available for public consumption whether you want to be or not."

"You think I don't know that?" I grumble, downing the rest of my beer in one swallow.

Peyton crosses her arms, keeping her hard eyes on me. "Then why am I here at midnight?"

I throw a few twenties on the bar to cover my tab and stalk out the back entrance I came in. "I don't need this shit."

Huffy steps follow me out the door into the empty alley.

"And you think I do?" Peyton shouts behind me. Her voice echoes around the space.

Before I can make it three steps to my car, Peyton grabs my arm and spins me around to face her. The safety lights illuminate her features.

I used to have every one of them memorized.

The soft wisps of hair that frame her face.

Eyelashes that kiss the tops of her cheeks.

The way her top lip juts out over her bottom lip.

I shake my head, trying to ignore the way her fingers feel as they dig into my bicep.

"Colin. This is my dream job. Do you think I want to be babysitting you?"

"I'm so sorry that I'm making this difficult for you." I roll my eyes, pulling my arm out of her reach. I don't need her touch fogging up my brain.

"I could be doing a million other things, but instead I have to keep you in line."

"Guess I'll be making you earn it then." There's no room to breathe in this tight space. No matter where I turn, I can smell the faint jasmine of Peyton's perfume.

I'd know that smell anywhere. Because I used to get it for her all the time.

I hate all these memories slamming into me. It's the last thing I need right now.

"Damn it, Colin! Can't you make this easy on me?" she screams in frustration.

"Easy on you? That's rich," I scoff.

"Do you have any idea what it's like? Having to comb through every article written about you and any jersey chaser you've been with?" I can see the hurt in her eyes. But the judgment in her tone has me lashing out.

"Fuck, Peyton. You don't get to judge me for decisions I made when you left."

Peyton rears back. "When I left? Fuck you, Colin! You were drafted and couldn't be bothered with your college sweetheart anymore."

This is the last thing we need to be doing in this alley. Taking out five years' worth of frustrations on each other.

But that's exactly what this is.

Frustration. Anger. Heartache.

She left without looking back, and it was the hardest fucking thing I've had to deal with in my life—getting over the woman I thought I was going to spend my life with.

Thank God I was drafted and came to Denver. It was my one saving grace.

I take a step closer to her. "Then if it's so hard, why don't you request a new assignment?"

We're almost chest to chest. Anger is wafting off both of us.

"And tell Earl, thanks for the opportunity, but I can't work with my ex? You'd love that, wouldn't you?"

"If it means no more back alley meet and greets, then yes."

Peyton tips her chin up to glare at me. I don't know how we got so close together.

"Too bad. I'm not going to let you scare me away."

"And here I thought it didn't take much to send you running."

"Screw you." Peyton shoves me away, but I catch her hand on my chest.

The tension between the two of us is at a breaking point. Peyton makes no move to pull her hand away from me. Our eyes are deadlocked.

I'm not sure who snaps first, but the next thing I know, our lips are crashing together. Both of us are fighting for control as our mouths meet for the first time in years.

It's new and familiar all at the same time.

I tug her bottom lip between my teeth. The soft gasp that escapes has my dick hardening in my pants before I attack her mouth again.

Fuck. I forgot how good she was at kissing. Her hands find my hair, tugging me just the way she likes.

I back her up against the brick wall, deepening the kiss. Needing to take more. I shouldn't want this. I shouldn't even be doing this, but fuck me.

I'm helpless.

This woman always drove me crazy with need. Even now, with so many twisted-up feelings toward her, I fall at her feet.

My lips drift down her jaw, nipping and sucking. All I'm thinking about is taking her home with me when I'm shoved backward.

Peyton's lips are swollen and her eyes are hazy with lust.

Fuck.

Fuck.

We shouldn't have done that. Now that the lust is clearing, anger fills in the void. I shouldn't want her. Not when everything is at stake.

"That can't happen again," Peyton whispers.

"It was a mistake," I agree.

"Good. Then I'll see you tomorrow?"

"I guess so."

I watch Peyton as she retreats to her car. And all I can think about is that kiss.

Fuck.

This is going to be the hardest few weeks of my life.

Chapter Seven

COLIN

"**D**o you remember everything we discussed?" Peyton is looking at something in her hand, not paying the slightest bit of attention to me. Instead of having me come into the office to discuss tonight's event, she emailed me the details.

With specific things not to do.

"Relax." I rest a hand on her shoulder out of instinct. "I've got this."

She shrugs me off, turning to look at me. "Everyone seems to think that this is a good idea—you being here at this event. But I'm still concerned. So I'm going to ask again…do you remember what we discussed?"

This time, Peyton's brows are furrowed in contempt. I don't think I've ever seen her like this. Well, at least toward me.

"Keep conversation light. Don't say anything about the article, and sign autographs and take selfies when asked."

Peyton blows out a breath, mumbling something I can't quite hear.

"Sorry, Rocky, didn't catch that."

"Please don't make this evening any more difficult than it has to be. Those women in there are some of the biggest supporters of the team, and I want this to go well. Be warm and gracious but not overly cocky."

"I got this, Peyton. You'll see."

I inject more confidence into my words than I'm actually feeling. Having every single one of your past indiscretions out there for everyone to know isn't the best feeling in the world. Especially when it's your ex pointing them out.

As I push open the doors into the meeting rooms, all eyes shift to me. It's hard not to feel their judgmental stares as I take in the Mountain Lions Women's Group before me. I've done a few of their events in previous seasons, but it's been awhile.

"Colin. How nice to see you." Maryanne, the director of the program, greets me.

"If it isn't one of my favorite ladies." I take her extended hand, relaxing somewhat. She's always been one of my favorites.

"I bet you say that to everyone."

I wink at her. "Only when it's true."

She swats at me with a perfectly manicured hand. "We have some new members that I'd like you to meet."

"Lead the way."

I can feel Peyton's presence behind me. I couldn't ignore her if I tried. Tension is drifting off her in waves. I knew working together would be rough, but she's a rubber band stretched to her breaking point. So tight, ready to snap.

"Ladies, I would like to introduce you to our star wide receiver, Colin James."

"Well, aren't you much cuter in person." A woman

with blonde hair, teased to within an inch of her life, looks me up and down. I've never felt so on display before.

"How's everyone doing tonight? Is this your first time here?" I ask, trying to be cordial.

"Lara is new." Maryanne points to the woman who spoke earlier. "She wants to be more involved in the community events the Mountain Lions host every year."

"That sounds great. We've got some good ones coming up this year."

It's one of the reasons I love Denver. The community involvement is something you don't see with a lot of teams. I love that the women's group hosts events and raises money for the different charities the Mountain Lions support.

"If you don't mind,"—Lara links her arm through mine—"I'd like to talk to you about a few ideas I have."

The sickly sweet tone of her voice puts me on edge. I have half a mind to decline, but Peyton's words from earlier echo in my head. *Be warm and gracious.*

"Have you been a Mountain Lions fan for a long time?" It's my go-to question in these situations.

"My *ex*-husband was a fan. It's how I got into the game," Lara answers.

God, I wish alcohol was served at these events. I don't miss the emphasis on her ex. This is the last thing I need right now.

"Hopefully we'll give you something to cheer for this season."

Lara lets out a shrill laugh, piercing my eardrums. "Listen to you. So modest. Of course it's going to be a great season. With these arms,"—she proceeds to squeeze my biceps—"you'll be catching touchdowns left and right."

"Alex is a great quarterback." I take a step back, trying

to put some distance between the two of us. "One of the best."

"Why didn't he come tonight?" She's looking around, hoping he might materialize out of thin air.

"Disappointed it's just me?"

This pulls her gaze down my body. Fuck. Being charming is a reflex I wish I could turn off.

"Sweetheart, I'm anything but disappointed." Lara looks around and then takes a step closer, shoving a giant set of tits in my face. No doubt bought by her ex. "Maybe you could take me back to your place tonight? I could see if all those articles about you are true."

"I'm sorry. Would you mind if I steal Colin away for a minute?" Peyton appears at my arm. Thank fuck.

"Oh sure thing. I was just getting to know him better." Lara runs a red-tipped nail down my arm. "Find me before you go. My offer still stands." She winks at me.

Peyton's grip on my arm is like a vise. It's the only thing that prevents me from fleeing like a dog with its tail between its legs.

"You need to stop flirting," Peyton whispers through clenched teeth, pulling me into a corner of the room away from the other guests.

"Not sure how much of that you caught, but that was definitely not me flirting with her."

"Sure sounded like it to me." Peyton crosses her arms.

I know exactly how I need to be acting tonight, but right now? I want to go toe-to-toe with Peyton. I'm sick of this ice-queen side of hers when it wasn't me in the wrong here.

"I can't exactly be a dick to these people. Sometimes a little harmless flirting is okay." I take in her defensive posture. "Why? Is it bothering you that I'm not flirting with you?"

Her laugh is sardonic. "Oh please. Like I'd be jealous of her."

My lips quirk up ever so slightly. Whether Peyton knows it or not, she's showing her cards. From the moment I met her here tonight, her walls have been up. It's like we never even met at the bar. "I never said jealous."

I don't miss the widening of her eyes or the pink coloring her cheeks. Busted.

"Did you want to be the one offering to take me home?" I shouldn't be throwing that in her face, but I'm over tonight.

"You cannot seriously be going home with that woman!" Peyton pokes a finger in my chest. "Do you know how bad that will look?"

"About as bad as leaving with you?"

"Damn it, Colin!" She shoves me back this time. "Why are you being like this? Can you not see how your actions have consequences?"

"I'm getting really tired of people pointing out how terrible I am." I crowd Peyton against the wall, doing little to hide the anger that is now filling me.

"I didn't say you were terrible."

I roll my eyes. "Technicality, Rocky."

"Don't call me that." The fire in her eyes matches mine. Her brown eyes are angry.

God. It reminds me of the first time we had sex while fighting. The push and pull. It's the same fiery gaze that she's aiming my way now. It makes me want to drag her into a room and feel her tight heat around me.

It's almost enough to distract me from her words.

Almost.

"Then don't tell me I'm a terrible person," I growl. I crowd in closer, causing Peyton to tip her chin up.

"I didn't say you were a terrible person." Her hand

drifts up my chest. No doubt she can feel the rapid beat of my heart. "Your actions are. Have you stopped to think beyond your dick?"

"And yet, it seems you should be thanking my dick."

Peyton huffs out a laugh. Her breath is hot against my skin. "Can we stop talking about your dick? God, the number of times I've had to discuss it!"

"You brought him up."

"Only because it got us into this mess!" Peyton hisses. "If you didn't feel the need to sleep with every woman you crossed paths with, I wouldn't be here right now!"

An emotion that looks an awful lot like sadness crosses her eyes. It's one of the things I always loved about Peyton. I could read her like a book.

"Is that why you hate me so much? Because it's not you I'm sleeping with?"

"It'd be easier if I did."

Her confession hits me square in the gut.

"Colin. Miss…" Maryanne walks over to us.

"Thompson." Peyton doesn't take her eyes off me. She's breathing fire. I wouldn't be surprised if steam came out of her ears. I take two steps back, putting some much-needed distance between the two of us.

"You're starting to draw some unwanted attention. Might we continue this conversation another time?"

"I'm so sorry, Maryanne. Please forgive me." Peyton runs a hand down her dress. The switch is flipped, and Peyton is back in professional mode.

I'm not as quick. Emotions are still warring in my chest.

Lust. Anger.

We said that one kiss was a mistake, but right now, I want a repeat of it. But I can't let it happen.

I won't let it happen.

Shaking the fog from my head, I mingle with the women, being perfectly charming and keeping a safe distance from Lara.

And Peyton.

Because she's the most dangerous woman of all here.

Chapter Eight

PEYTON

"How are things going with Colin?" Grier asks, knocking back the shot she ordered. "We're allowed to say his name now, right? Now that you're working with him?"

I take my shot, enjoying a night out together. "Yes. You can say his name. Things are going."

"That sounds juicy." She rubs her hands together, obviously wanting more detail.

I suck on the lime, biting back the taste of tequila. "Everything has been so hot and cold. I have no idea where I stand with him. I want to keep things professional, but he keeps looking at me."

"Heaven forbid, he looked at you!" Grier overexaggerates a gasp. "How dare he!"

"Shut up!" I laugh. "You know what I mean."

"Loaded and filled with meaning?"

"Yes! I want to keep things professional, but he's making it hard."

"I bet you're making him hard." Grier waggles her eyebrows at me.

I chuck my lime wedge at her. "I can't take you anywhere!"

"You set it up for me. How could I leave it dangling?" She laughs.

"Maybe you just need to get laid."

"Know any hot football players?"

Hot jealousy cuts through me in a flash. There is no way Grier would ever go after Colin, but just the thought of it has me wanting to put up a fight for my guy.

Except he's not my guy. Not anymore.

"Calm down, girl. I didn't mean Colin."

"See? This is what I'm talking about!" I slap my hands over my eyes. "I want him, but I can't want him. Why is being an adult so difficult?"

"I think you're making it harder on yourself." Grier signals to the bartender for another round, adding margaritas to the mix.

"I could lose my job if I start anything with Colin. I can't lose this opportunity."

"Easy. Don't start anything then." Grier takes one of the drinks set in front of her and passes it to me. "Why? Is anything starting? Did I miss something?"

Heat floods my cheeks. Grier's eyes go wide the minute she notices.

"Spill, girl."

"We kissed."

"You kissed?" she shrieks, letting the whole bar around us know what happened.

"Oh my God. Could you be any louder?"

"I'm sorry." She holds up a hand, interrupting herself. "You kissed the man who broke your heart in college. How else am I supposed to react?"

"It was a one-time thing. It can't happen again."

"But you want it to." Grier drags a finger through the salt on the rim of her margarita.

"Yes. No. I don't know. God, the man is infuriating."

"So bang it out and be done." She wipes her hands like that's the end of the problem.

"Thank you for putting that into my brain."

"You two would make such pretty babies."

I groan at her words. While Grier knows about a lot of things that happened between Colin and me during school, she doesn't know this. It wasn't something I wanted to tell.

"You really aren't helping. Why am I friends with you?" I laugh, bringing my thoughts back to a safer place.

"Your life would be so boring without me."

"I'd take that quiet existence right about now. No Colin to worry about or a job to stress about getting."

Colin and I are practically two strangers now, trying to navigate the minefield we created between us. Because that's exactly what it is. The smallest wrong step could have far-reaching consequences for both of us.

Colin could get traded. Any future career I want in sports could be cut off at the knees before I even have a chance to try.

"Earth to Peyton." Grier snaps her fingers in front of me.

"Sorry." I shake my head, trying to dislodge the cobwebs that have taken over.

"Damn. You're really torn up about this."

I rest my hand in my chin on the bar. "Maybe I just need to do some more shots with you and it'll make everything better."

Her laughter eases the tight feeling in my chest. "I don't know if shots will make you feel better. But it'll definitely make you forget."

"Let's not go crazy." I lift my glass up to hers, clinking it in a cheers before downing the icy-cold liquid.

"You can push through this for a few more months. Just think of the end goal. A job working for one of the best teams in the NFL. Or with Earl's company."

"God. It's all I've ever wanted."

"And you'd be stupid to give it up for some guy," Grier states.

I straighten my shoulders. "You're right. Colin didn't think twice about giving me up in college, so why should I worry about him?"

Grier holds her hand up for a high five, which I answer with enthusiasm. "Damn straight, girl. Any man who ditches you isn't worth the pain."

"I'm incredible. Any guy would be lucky to have me."

"And me!" Grier chirps. "We're fucking catches."

"We are. We should only be looking forward, not backward."

"You're going to crush this internship, get a fantastic job, and have your pick of any guy out there."

I know Colin shouldn't be the one popping into my head, but he does. And it takes everything I have to push down that feeling of wanting him. Because this is the kind of energy I need.

Focusing on my internship, graduating, and getting the dream job.

The dream guy has come and gone for me. My only focus these last few years has been on getting what I've always wanted. Sure, a few guys have been in the picture along the way, but no one who made me want to take my eyes off the prize.

Colin's reentry into my life shouldn't change that. It *can't* change that.

"You're right. These next few months are going to be incredible. I can feel it."

Grier beams at me. "And just in case you need the reminder, don't sleep with Colin."

Easier said than done.

COLIN

"Do I really have to do this?" I adjust the cuffs of my shirt for what feels like the eighth time tonight.

"The question you should be asking is why you dragged all of us into this mess," Knox growls.

"Hey!" I throw my hands up in defense. "It seemed like a good idea at the time."

"Right. I seem to recall you saying it might be a good way to 'meet hot chicks.'" Knox quirks a brow in my direction, daring me to argue with him.

"That…is entirely true. Fuck." Scrubbing a hand down my face, I will time to move faster.

"You just need a drink. This is going to be awesome!" Logan hands me a glass of bourbon, and I knock it back in one swallow.

"You know you're not allowed to sleep with your date for the evening, right?" Alex pins him with a fierce stare. "This is to raise money for the new cancer wing at the children's hospital."

"Relax. He knows," Knox chimes in.

"Yeah, sure thing." Logan's face is a dead giveaway. He's hoping to nail whoever wins him tonight.

"I'm surprised charity date auctions are still a thing." I hold my glass out toward Jackson, having him top me off.

"Apparently the team's social media coordinator knows someone at the hospital. And because you can't keep your dick in your pants,"—Knox glares at me—"you can't get any bad press by canceling on a children's hospital. So yes, you really do have to do this, and it is your fault."

"How'd you get roped into this, Fields?" I nod toward Jackson. Ever since he got married, we barely see him.

"A night out with Tenley benefiting a good cause? She was all about it." He gets that dopey smile that only she can put on his face.

"Are you guys ready?" Peyton pops her head into the waiting area backstage. While she wasn't crazy about my participating in this, Knox was right that I really couldn't cancel my commitment, so she insisted on becoming involved in the auction to keep me out of trouble.

"Let's get this over with." Alex sounds about as excited as I do to be here tonight.

"You guys will do great. A few of the other guys have already gone for the big bucks. You're doing something great here. Just remember to smile."

Peyton aims those last words at me.

"What? People love me!"

The stare she gives me could melt glass. "Yes, and my presence here is because the people love you so much."

"Fuck. Colin's babysitter came to play!" Knox grabs me by the shoulders. "You do not want to mess with her."

Those big brown eyes of hers never leave mine. Her face doesn't change at Knox's words. "Can I please have a word with Colin?"

"Someone's in trouble," one of the guys whispers as they skate out of the room.

Peyton rounds on me as soon as the door clicks shut behind her. "Can you take something in your life seriously? Just once?"

"I'm here, aren't I?" I spread my arms out around me.

She takes a step closer. With her heels on, she's almost at eye level with me. Her arms brush against my chest, sending a shock of heat rippling through me. I know I shouldn't, but I like this feisty side of Peyton. I always got the caring, loving side in college. This is new.

And I don't hate it.

"You're here because you made a commitment, and because you'll do anything to get back into the good graces of the team."

I start to interrupt, but she holds up a finger.

"I don't want to hear it. You need to be the boy next door, not the guy sneaking out of the window. If you are anything less than the charming man I know you can be out there, this will not end well for you."

Ouch. Peyton's words cut me. But she's not wrong.

"Okay—" A finger to my lips cuts me off.

"Don't argue with me."

Grabbing her wrist, I pull her hand down and into my chest. Heat swirls between the two of us in the small room. The pulse in her wrist throbs. Her pupils widen as her gaze flicks to my lips. Peyton is inches from me.

It'd be so easy to take. To dip my lips down and take hers in a kiss I now know she wants. To pin her against the wall and remember what her curves feel like under my fingers.

It'd be so easy.

I'd done it before in a heated moment. Much like this one.

As much as I want to act on this sudden flash of want, she would knee me in the balls faster than I could blink.

I take a step back. And then another.

"I wasn't going to argue."

"Good." Peyton pulls her hand from my grasp and straightens her skirt. When her eyes meet mine again, they mean business. All emotion is locked down and hidden away. "Now get out there and charm those people into spending their evening with you."

"You got it, Rocky."

"DO I HEAR FIVE THOUSAND DOLLARS?" The auctioneer bellows from his place at the mic, and a woman in the front row raises her paddle.

Peyton wasn't kidding when she said people were shelling out big bucks for a date with the team tonight.

"How about six thousand?" I shield my eyes from the lights shining on the stage, trying to see if anyone else is going to bid.

"Going once…going twice…sold!" He bangs his gavel as a whoop is heard from the crowd.

I rush off the stage to see Peyton standing with the guys and a few other members from the team.

"You have to take it back!" Knox groans.

"Why? It was the best bid of the night." Peyton is downright playful as I join their conversation. For once, it's an easy smile when she looks at me.

"What's going on?" I ask.

"My grandma bid on you," Knox bemoans.

"Did she win?" I ask. Thank God I don't have a drink; otherwise, it'd be spewed out all over the place.

"Why else would I be this upset? You can't take my grandma out!" he hisses.

"Will she get handsy?"

"I swear to God, Colin—" Fury pulsates off of Knox.

"Well, well, well. If it isn't my prize for the evening." A woman with wrinkles lining her face and a helmet of gray hair greets us. "Knox, be a dear and introduce us."

I love this woman already.

"Colin, this is my grandma, Darlene." I can hear his teeth clank together at the rage of him having to introduce us. "Darlene, this is Colin. Apparently, your date."

"Aren't you a handsome young fella," Darlene purrs.

"Not handsome enough to win over someone like you." Charm oozes off my words.

"Oh, you're good. Knox, why didn't you introduce us sooner?" She doesn't take her playful eyes off me.

"This is your fault. You should have let him cancel." Knox shoots a disparaging look Peyton's way.

"Blame Colin. It's his fault for agreeing to participate." But the smile lighting up her face tells me she's loving this almost as much as I am.

Knox scrubs a hand down his face. "Grandma. You have to behave."

"Behaving is no fun." She sticks her lip out to him in a pout. "Now, Colin. How do you feel about bingo?"

Chapter Ten

COLIN

"**D**on't make me regret this." Knox gives me a hard stare, one I'm used to at this point. If Knox wants to come off like the bad boy of the team, then I'll let him have it.

"Your grandma invited me as her date. Clearly she loves me enough to play bingo with her."

Knox huffs as he pulls open the door to the retirement center where his grandma lives. "And I'm beginning to question her mental capacity."

"She has a soft spot for star receivers." I give him my most charming smile. "Maybe she needs a sugar daddy."

"I swear to fucking God, Colin…" The look Knox gives me would take down a lesser man, but the grandma in question is already waiting for us.

"Knox. Wipe that look off your face. You look constipated."

"Jesus, Grandma."

"Hi, Darlene. I'm so happy you invited me today." I lean into the open arms she's holding out for me. The biggest grin is on my face.

"I regret everything about this already," Knox whines.

Darlene waves him off, linking her arm with mine and pulling me along with her. "Ignore my grandson. He can be very moody."

"Oh, I do most days."

"Good, good. Now, are you ready for bingo?"

"Am I ready? I dusted off my bingo skills just for you." I'm laying it on thick, but I don't care. Darlene tells it like it is, and it's refreshing.

"Bingo is just luck," Knox grumbles.

I pull out a chair at the table for Darlene and lean down to her. "Was he like this growing up?"

A whack to the head tells me I might've gone a step too far.

"There will be no embarrassing childhood stories told today." Knox points at his grandma. "I'm serious."

She waves him off. "Fine. Then get your cute butt over here so we can start the game."

Knox, finally looking happy, sits next to Darlene. "Will Betty be joining us?"

Darlene cackles. "Oh no. She and Roy had a little accident, if you know what I mean."

"What do you mean?" I naively ask.

"For fuck's sake."

"They had a little too much fun in bed, and Betty threw out a hip."

Laughter bursts out of me. "Knox, I love your grandma!"

Growing up, my parents weren't close to their parents, and after my parents divorced, I rarely saw them. To get to hang out with Darlene today is something I didn't realize I missed growing up. And even if it's just for today, I soak it up for all that it's worth.

"Grandma! Seriously, can you act your age for once?" Knox's face is bright red as bingo cards are passed around.

"Darling, when was the last time I ever minced my words?"

Knox mumbles to himself as the game starts.

"I-27."

"Colin. Tell me about this lady friend of yours." Darlene isn't looking at me as she asks the questions.

"Lady friend?"

"Yes. The pretty one from the event. She was looking at you like the tall drink of water that you are."

That's news to me. Because if Peyton is looking at me with anything other than contempt these days, I'd die of shock.

"Umm, fine, I guess."

"Fine? Lord have mercy, no wonder both you boys are alone."

"Hey, we're talking about him, not me," Knox says in defense.

"Don't think I'm not paying attention, Knox." Darlene wags a finger at him. "I'm biding my time, waiting on great-grandbabies from you. But Colin here seems to find himself in more of a pickle."

"I mean, things could be going better."

"B-7."

"Did Knox here give you any advice? He used to be quite the ladies' man."

"What do you mean used to be?" Knox quirks a brow in his grandma's direction, placing a bingo chip on his board.

"Like I said, I don't see any great-grandbabies running around here, do I?"

I cannot contain my laughter around this woman,

drawing the attention of people around us. "Darlene, you're my favorite."

"As I should be." She prods me with a bony finger. "And I bet that cute face of yours gets you far in life."

"That would be a fair statement." I shrug my shoulders, covering another space as numbers get called out around us.

"It's all I want for my Knoxy here." She pats him on the cheek. "I know he loves football, but I wouldn't mind him bringing a nice young lady around here."

"I'll work on it. Just for you, Grandma." Knox drops a kiss on her cheek.

I feel a tug in my chest, watching these two together. The closest thing I ever had to family like this was Peyton's family. They welcomed me with open arms.

But as soon as I left school for the draft, any sense of family left me when she did. It's something I've always wished for. I feel a jealous ache for this kind of love from another person. Because watching Knox with his grandma makes me want this too.

Growing up, I spent most of my time with my dad. Summers were spent at sleepaway football camps, and the rest of the year with the best trainers money could buy. I didn't get much love from my dad. And the only attention I got from him was if my playing suffered.

"You're not paying attention to your board. Don't think I'll give you all the numbers," Darlene pipes up.

I laugh. "I wouldn't dream of it."

"Now, back to your lady."

"Why does everyone need a say in my love life?"

"Because you're doing it wrong," Darlene and Knox say at the same time.

Knox, being the bastard that he is, has his arms

crossed, leaning back in his chair. His amusement is written on his face, plain as day.

I let Darlene drone on about all the ways I can win someone over.

"G-53!"

"Ha! Bingo!" Darlene shouts.

"You're cheating! No way you have bingo!" someone yells from behind us.

"Uh-oh," Knox mutters as Darlene spins in her chair.

"How can you cheat in bingo? I have all the numbers he called. Right, Colin?" She twists in the seat to look at me. The look says don't you dare disagree.

"That's right." I nod. "She has all the numbers he's called."

"Good boy," Darlene says, patting me on the cheek. "Knox, you can bring him back here anytime."

"I'd love that."

Darlene takes the lottery ticket prize from the announcer after he checks her board.

"And who knows, maybe next time you'll both be bringing your girlfriends with you."

Chapter Eleven

COLIN

"Why did you think this was a good idea?"

Peyton rolls her eyes at me. "They're just kids, Colin. You'll be fine."

Easy for her to say. She wasn't about to read a book to what seems like fifty kids.

"Hey Colin. You ready to get started?" Tenley appears next to us. Jackson is right beside her.

"I mean, I guess."

Tenley gives me a bright smile. It doesn't do anything to quell my nerves. "You'll do great, I promise. They love it when the football players come in and read to them."

"They love it when I do it," Jackson quips.

"Seriously, Jackson?" Tenley looks like she wants to smack him. "Colin, if these kids can love this grump,"— she swats at Jackson— "then they'll love you. I picked out their favorite book for you to read to them."

"Okay. Let's get started."

Tenley starts to gather the students as they're running around the room. "Are you really sure I can do this, Peyton?"

I don't think I've ever been this nervous before. Not even before my first NFL game. Football games you know what's coming. Kindergartners? Hell no.

Peyton's brown eyes pierce straight into me. "Colin, I wouldn't sign you up to do this if I didn't think you could do it. You have the personality and charm to win these kids over. Talk to them. Answer their questions. They'll love you." Peyton gives me an encouraging smile. Her hand squeezes my bicep.

It's what I need. It settles the ball of nerves in my stomach.

Peyton has always been the one person who could. She was my good luck charm before every game in college. I'd be a nervous wreck if it weren't for her.

"Alright, everyone. I know Mr. Jackson usually reads to you on Fridays, but he brought along a friend of his. Can everyone say hi to Mr. Colin?"

"Hi, Mr. Colin." Voices echo around the room. Twenty sets of eyes are staring up at me.

I can do this.

"Hi, everyone." I give a nervous wave and fight the urge to flinch. My eyes find Peyton, now in the back of the room. She gives me an encouraging thumbs-up.

I can do this.

"So, what are we reading today?"

I take the seat that Tenley has set up for me in front of the room. Eager hands shoot up into the air. I point to a little boy in the front.

"*Cloudy with a Chance of Meatballs!*"

"Right!" I try to act more excited than I actually am. I don't want to scare these kids off before I even get started.

I open the first pages of the book and start reading. The kids are hooked on my every word. Their giggles at certain parts of the book have a genuine smile spreading across my face. When I get to the part about a pancake falling on the school, hands rise into the air. I don't even have a chance to call on them before they're shouting out questions.

"What would happen if a pancake fell on our school and we were inside?"

"How big would a pancake have to be to cover our school?"

"Can we have pancakes for lunch?"

Fuck, these kids are cute. I can see why Jackson likes doing this so much. Forget the fact that his wife is the teacher, but this is fun.

"Well, how do you think we'd get out of the school if a pancake fell on it?" I ask them.

I can see the wheels spinning in their tiny heads.

"Could we eat our way out?" a little voice in the back pipes up. "But we might get a tummy ache."

"Well, if we all ate a little bit, do you think we'd make a hole big enough to squeeze through?" I ask.

"You're a big kid. Can you just push through it?" someone in the front asks.

I can't help the laugh that escapes. I bring my arm up, showing off my arms. "You think I could break through a pancake?"

Peyton is in the back of the room taking pictures as the kids squeal in delight.

"Mrs. Fields! Can we make a pancake and see if Mr. Colin can break through it?"

"I don't know, that seems like an awfully big pancake," Tenley chimes in. "How would we make one?"

The kids run off on another tangent. Jackson is laughing, listening to them as I sneak a peek at Peyton. Her eyes are fixed on me. There's a softness there that I haven't seen in a long time.

The last few weeks, it's mostly been annoyance. I'm not an idiot. I know this assignment wasn't what she wanted. I'm standing between her and her dream job.

But that look she's giving me? It's one I recognize. When I had a bad game, it was the one telling me it was okay and I could lean on her. Peyton was my safe place. Being a college football star wasn't easy. The grab for attention from everyone was too much some days.

I realize now that being here with her—and about twenty kindergartners—there's nowhere else I'd rather be.

"Why did we have to schlep ourselves all the way out to the burbs?" Logan looks around my house in awe as he steps in the front door. The open floor plan is spacious, with refinished hardwood floors and a kitchen most chefs would dream of.

"Because I've been told I shouldn't be seen out, even with you guys." I shut the door behind the guys. With the bad press I've been getting, Earl thought it best for me to lie low outside of any scheduled events. So instead of hitting our usual preseason bar, the boys came over to my place for drinks.

"Let's just hope we don't jinx ourselves by not going to the Book Bar." Alex claps me on my shoulder as he heads outside. He's been here a few times in the past. We forged an easy bond, and we've only grown closer over the years.

"Dude. Don't put that bad mojo out into the world." I shrug him off and follow his lead. Knox and Jackson have already made themselves comfortable outside on the couch in front of the firepit.

It's cool for a summer night. The perfect evening

before our season kicks off this week. With everything going on, the season starting snuck up on me.

"Even I know that!" Logan says, grabbing a beer from the outdoor fridge on my patio. It was one of the selling points of this house. That and the gated community to keep the women out.

"I'm back this year and feeling better than ever, so we'll be fine." Jackson points his beer bottle in my direction.

"Damn. Being in a relationship has made you downright sappy."

A sly smile washes over his face. "You guys should try it. Feels pretty fucking good."

I'd hate him if he wasn't one of my best friends. He was a sad sack without Tenley last year—even for only a few weeks—and now they're married.

"What if I said I had someone? Potentially."

"What? Since when?" Knox pops a pretzel in his mouth as he leans back in his chair. The sun is setting over the mountains in the distance. You can't beat this view.

I debate how much I want to tell them. It's not like Peyton and I can act on any feelings we might have. Well, me. But after being with her at Tenley's school, I think that icy wall of hers is starting to thaw.

"She knew me before all this." I wave my hand around me. "We dated in college. I thought I was going to marry her."

"No shit," Alex says, shaking his head. "What happened?"

"Things got pretty serious, and then I got a letter from her before the draft saying she couldn't see me anymore. That everything in my life would be too crazy and she couldn't handle it."

Anger burns hot in my chest. I never let go of it, what she did to me. I turned it into fuel on the football field.

"And you want to start things up with her again?" Alex asks.

I shrug my shoulders. "It's not like I ever stopped loving her."

"You guys are worse gossips than my sisters." Logan shakes his head.

"No one said you have to keep coming to these." Knox shoves Logan's feet off the wall of the firepit.

Logan's face loses all color. "No!" He clears his throat. "I mean, I like coming to these things."

"Give him a break, Fisher." Alex swats at Knox. "Maybe trying something with her would be a good thing?"

"I can't."

"Aww, poor baby can't get it up anymore?" Knox gives me a smug grin. "No wonder she left you."

"You're a dick." I throw a pretzel at him. He easily catches it and pops it in his mouth. "Let's just say it wouldn't look good if we were together."

"You can never make things easy on yourself, can you?" Alex says. Logan, Jackson and Knox drift off into their own conversation.

"Where's the fun in that?" I quirk my lips up before taking a sip of my beer. Between that and the fire, it's the perfect preseason night. Even if we can't be at our local haunt, being with the guys who have become brothers to me makes up for it.

"Would there even be the possibility of you two getting back together?" Alex shifts forward, resting his forearms on his knees, his beer bottle dangling between his fingers.

Peyton came back into my life in the most unexpected of ways. I never actually expected to ever see her again. I went from college to the draft to Denver in the span of a few weeks. I never finished my degree. Life became all about football.

And women. Anything to dull the ache of losing her.

"Honestly? I don't know." I pick at the crinkled label on my beer bottle. "We were everything to each other, and now she can't even stand to be in the same room with me."

"Can you really blame her when you show up on TMZ more than any other celebrity?"

"Hey!" I whack him on the arm. "I haven't shown up on any gossip blogs in at least a few weeks."

"You need a pat on the back?" Alex chides.

"Fuck you very much!" I flip him off.

"So make her see that you've changed. Why would she want to get back together with you when all she sees is you chasing after every woman out there?"

"And how do I do that, oh wise one?" I roll my eyes as I rock back into the sofa.

"Fields. Help a guy out." Alex's tone is commanding as he pulls Jackson into the conversation.

"What's up?" He leans into our conversation as everyone quiets down. Alex has that way about him.

"Colin needs helping wooing someone."

"Wooing?" Jackson barks out a laugh. Alex only has to raise an eyebrow and it has him shutting his mouth. "Right. What do you need help with?"

Mulling it over, I try to think of a way to word it without giving away who it is. Because if these guys knew I was trying to win over the woman digging me out of this hole I found myself in, they wouldn't be so encouraging.

"Contrary to what the media believes, I wasn't always such a ladies' man."

"You mean man-whore," Knox deadpans.

"Don't think I won't kick you out of my house."

Knox points at Alex. "This is why the bar is sacred. No one actually has the power to kick anyone out."

"Back to the point at hand, what does your girl like?" Jackson asks, a seriousness to his tone.

"Football. Camping. Mexican food." I smile at the picture of Peyton I have in my mind. She was always the first one up for any adventure in college.

Hiking in the Smokies? She's there.

Football in the quad at midnight? Any day of the week.

"Show her you still remember what she likes. Don't act like a dick."

"Easier said than done." Logan laughs to himself.

"Hey." Jackson is all business. "I'm serious. If you don't show any interest in what she likes, then what chance do you have of your relationship going anywhere?"

"I knew he'd have the answer," Alex whispers to me.

"So take her hiking after a football game and then have tacos for dinner," Knox snickers.

"You're such a jackass." Jackson smacks him upside the head.

"How am I more mature than he is?" Logan points to Knox.

"No one said you were," Alex replies. "Maybe don't listen to those two."

"It won't be easy with the season starting, but you can figure something out," Jackson says.

"Fuck man, when did you become so smart?" I take a long pull of my beer.

"About the time I fucked up my leg and needed Tenley. If I didn't get my shit together, do you think we'd be having a baby together?"

Jackson's words have all of our mouths dropping in shock.

I recover first. "Are you for real?"

The dopiest grin washes over his face. "Yes. But you guys can't tell anyone! She'd kill me if she knew I told people. It's still early."

We all clamber up, pulling him into a group hug, shouting to be heard.

"That's awesome!"

"Congrats!"

"Are you able to be a parent when you're not a grown-up yourself?"

Jackson whacks Logan's head at his words. "More qualified than you."

I once thought that might've been my future, but it wasn't. Now, Peyton and I are in this weird place. I don't miss the sidelong glances she sends my way. And every time we work together, I see her facade cracking.

Instead of stewing on what Peyton and I could have been, I am brought back to the present by Alex clearing his throat and saying, "Well, I guess this is as good of a time as any then for my toast, boys." We all raise our drinks.

"Let me start by saying congrats, Jackson. You and Tenley are going to be the best parents, and hopefully raise better people than we are football players."

Jackson gives him a genuine smile. "God, I hope so."

"And I know last year wasn't the season we wanted. But this year? I can feel it. Jackson is back."

The guys break out into cheers.

"We've been together for the last few years and know the playbook better than anyone else. We're captains for a reason."

Alex pins each of us with a stare. It's his quarterback stare. The one that can scare opposing defenses with his precision in picking them apart.

"We've got what it takes. It won't be easy. We know that. But we can do it. We fight for every yard. Every point.

Every win." There's a fire in his speech, one that settles inside of me and ignites the same passion for the game. "I don't want to be sitting on the sidelines again next January."

Everyone straightens at Alex's words. We know the stakes. Every football player out there wants to be going to the playoffs. It hurts when you miss out. Especially when you have the talent to go far.

"I wouldn't want to go into battle with anyone else but you boys. We have each other's backs, win or lose."

Alex raises his bottle. "To the Mountain Lions and having the best season we can have."

I look at each man standing next to me. These men are more than my teammates. They're my best friends. My brothers. My chosen family. We all have the same hungry gleam in our eyes.

We don't want to only make it to the playoffs. We want to go to the big game. To the Super Bowl. It's all we ever dreamed about when we were playing peewee football.

Denver has put together the best team in years. Each of us here, and those that aren't, are ready. Ready for the first snap of the ball. That first whistle as we tear down the field. To feel the dirt under our fingers as we make a play.

Everyone clinks their drink to Alex's.

"To the Mountain Lions!"

Chapter Thirteen

PEYTON

"Miss Myers. I'm so glad you could make it today."

"Call me Audrey." The blonde bombshell in front of me flashes a blindingly white smile. "I'm so happy that Earl and the Mountain Lions worked this out."

"They were very grateful you could come."

When Earl called me to handle this today because Denver's Communications Director was out, I jumped at the chance. Getting to meet a badass Olympian who calls Denver home?

I'd be stupid not to take that chance.

"Is it weird that I'm nervous?" She wrings her hands in front of her.

"You ski down some of the highest mountains in the world and 76,000 fans scare you?" I laugh.

She holds up her hands in defense. "I'd gladly take that mountain any day. Football fans are a completely different beast."

A commotion behind us pulls our attention away from each other. The team bus has arrived, and players start tunneling down the concrete hall toward the locker room.

"Is it bad I'm checking them all out?" Audrey whispers to me.

I don't notice a single player. My eyes are darting around, trying to find the one I really want to see. Men tower over us. A few wave to Audrey, but my eyes only connect with Colin's.

A smile pulls at the corner of his lips. The first flutters of butterflies release in my stomach. Ever since we went to Tenley's class, something has shifted between us. It's like whatever tension there was between us was sucked out of the room.

He doesn't spare a glance at Audrey. His eyes are zeroed in on me as he breaks away and runs over.

"I didn't realize you'd be here today." Colin's smile is bright now.

"Earl had me step in with Audrey here. She'll be the honorary captain doing the coin toss."

"Hi, Audrey. Colin James." Colin extends a hand to Audrey. Her gaze rakes over him, and I fight the jealousy churning in my gut.

"Nice to meet you. I'm excited to be here," Audrey chimes.

"The crowd will love you." His smile is sincere. It's almost as if he doesn't notice the effect he has on her. "Can I talk to you?"

Colin grabs my elbow, pulling me away from Audrey.

"What's up?" I shake him off, ignoring the way sparks zinged up my arm at the slightest contact.

Chemistry was never the problem between us. It burned hot and bright, like an exploding star. And then swallowed us up into a black hole.

"Why does something need to be up?" Colin crowds in closer to me, crossing his arms over his chest.

"You said you needed to talk."

"Can't a guy just want a minute alone with you?"

That zing of electricity is pulsing between us. "Shouldn't you be focusing on the game?"

A smile lights up his face.

"Do you remember our pregame ritual?"

I cannot contain my laughter. "Oh my God. I can't believe I forgot."

"How could you forget our own game of x's and o's?" Colin shakes his head at me, his brown hair flopping into his eyes.

"I don't think I've looked at a playbook in years."

The way Colin's eyes soften tells me we both know the last time I looked at a playbook. I'm glad we can contain our feelings right now and not dissolve into frustrated anger.

"Studying plays was always more fun with you, Rocky."

For the first time in a long time, I smile at his nickname for me, fingering the necklace with the same name on it.

"Because you got a kiss for every play you got right," I say with a laugh.

I remember it like it was yesterday. It started after our first date. Colin thought he had the playbook memorized. We went back to his dorm room and I quizzed him on every play. What started as a game turned into a frantic make-out session.

But when the team won that weekend, Colin told me we had to do it again.

Not that any person would mind his lips on them. It was a hard job, but someone had to do it.

"Meant I got every play down pat."

"Colin!" Someone barks his name from behind us. "Let's go! We need to get out on the field for warm-ups."

The sense of loss that he has to leave is palpable. His brows pull together. "Will I see you after the game?"

I nod my head. "Earl got me tickets to his suite. I'll be here for the whole game."

"Great. I'll see you after." Colin starts to walk away, then turns to where Audrey is standing nearby, chatting with another player. "Logan, dude, drag yourself away and let's get going!"

I watch Colin's retreating form, trying to quell the nerves in my belly. Ever since he came crashing back into my life, I've been fighting the pull I've been feeling toward him.

Colin left. He got drafted by Denver and never looked back, leaving me at school by myself, with every plan we'd ever made, every whisper of love to each other, crushed into dust.

It took everything I had in me to piece myself back together after he left. A few guys came and went, but none of them were Colin.

And now that we're back in each other's lives, I'm feeling things for him that I thought were buried.

Feelings that could get me in trouble.

Pushing those rising feelings back down, I head back to Audrey, focusing on the job ahead.

As long as I keep my nose to the grindstone, I'll be okay.

I can only hope it's not the biggest lie I've ever told.

Chapter Fourteen

COLIN

"You ready to go, man?" I slap Knox on the shoulder.

"Fuck yeah!" He slaps two fists into my pads.

The first game of the season is here. And it's what we all live for—the rush as we run out onto the field to the crowd roaring our names.

And now that I know Peyton is here? I want to have the best game I've had in a long time.

I'm not above wanting to impress her. Now that the weird tension between us is down to a low simmer, I want to remind her why she fell for me in the first place.

"Think I can break one hundred yards?" I pull the jersey over my head.

"Dude, don't jinx yourself." Logan throws a towel in my direction.

I shake my head, chuckling at him. "Last season I had ninety-nine yards in the first game. Season before that, eighty-one. I'm ready to break a hundred."

"I'll be happy to start a game," Logan bemoans.

"You'll get there, kid." Alex claps him on the shoulder.

"I didn't start until my second season, and that's only because our quarterback went down."

I wince. I remember that hit. Ended his career in one play. Something you never want to see happen.

"I didn't start until my second season. Gotta earn it kid," I tell him.

"I know," Logan grumbles. "Can't really complain when our running back was at the top of the league last year."

Coach Brooks stands in the front of the room. "Alright boys, bring it in."

Everyone quiets down immediately. When Coach talks, we listen.

"First game of the season. Nothing like getting to start the season in front of the home crowd. Chicago is a good team. It won't be easy, but if we work our game plan, I know we'll be able to come out with a win today."

The air is alive in the room. The energy is palpable. Adrenaline is pumping through my veins. I know I'm not alone. Looking around, guys are antsy, shifting side to side on their feet.

"But we can't stop there. We need to keep building. We've got a great team. I know we can go all the way. So stick together. Drown out the outside noise and focus on each other. On being a team. A family. Because that will lead us to our ultimate goal."

Coach nods to Alex.

"You heard Coach!" Alex bellows, stepping into the center of the room. The team surges forward. "Let's go out there and show Chicago what we're made of and bring home the win. Family on three. One, two, three…"

"Family!" everyone echoes.

One by one, the locker room empties as the team funnels out toward the field.

The stadium is rocking. This place is like a second home—the black-and-yellow team colors always welcoming us here. I fucking love it.

We made the decision today that instead of the starting offensive line running out one by one, the entire team would run out together. We're ready to start this season together.

Everyone is fired up as we run out onto the field. Fireworks are exploding overhead as the crowd roars for us. It's deafening.

This is what I live for.

Alex starts his warm-up, tossing me the ball as the field clears for the coin toss. "You ready to go?"

"Hell yeah!" I hand the ball to the backup QB, and he throws it back to Alex.

Coach yells that it's time for the coin toss, but Alex pulls me back.

"Knox and Jackson are going out with Audrey for the flip."

The guys are laughing with her as they walk out to meet the opposing team's captains. Everyone shakes hands before the coin is tossed. The crowd cheers for Audrey as Chicago calls it.

They win it and defer to the second half.

Perfect.

I want to get out there and show everyone that I'm still the same old me. The one that can catch the perfect spiral for a touchdown.

Not the guy that went out to clubs every week and hooked up with any woman who looked his way.

"Alright, offense. Let's go. Good strong drive to open the game." Alex slaps my helmet as we run onto the field.

Immediately the crowd noise falls away. Alex has these

fans trained. Whenever the offense is on the field, it's so quiet you can hear a pin drop in the stands.

We don't huddle up, getting into our positions. We've had the first play of the game ready for weeks. With a new offensive coordinator joining the team this off-season, we wanted to be ready for a strong start.

"Black Fifty-two. Black Fifty-two. Set, hut!" The center snaps the ball, and I run a crossing route. Bypassing the safety that's on me, I zip horizontally across the field. With the other receivers drawing the safeties downfield, I'm open for Alex to throw me the ball.

It's a quick dart. I take off running, heading into the open field before I'm hit by a corner and eating dirt.

But not before I get the first down.

The crowd is going crazy.

Pulling a chunk of grass out of my helmet, I jog back toward the line.

"Great catch." Alex thwacks me on the head as I take my position.

This is what I live for. The grass beneath my feet. The crowd noise feeding the buzzing in my blood. My teammates clapping me on the back after a great catch.

God, I love football.

"Apple Eighty-five, break on one." Alex calls the run play.

I make my move as I watch the running back break free down the field. He gets down into the red zone before he gets tackled.

Alex doesn't give them a chance to sub out and gets us to the line fast. I barely hear the play before the ball is snapped.

Running down into the end zone, I see the ball soaring through the air to me. The corner is right on top of me. I can already tell the ball is overthrown.

Stretching up, I push myself that extra half step to haul it in. I drag my toes right on the line. The refs' arms reach up to the sky—touchdown.

All the guys are yelling and jumping around me. A touchdown on the opening drive of the first game of the season?

Damn, that felt good.

"Did you see that?" I holler, hugging Alex as he comes over to me. "Fuck, yeah!"

"Out here making me look good," he says as he laughs.

"Someone has to." I toss the ball back to the ref as Jackson runs onto the field for the extra point.

"Great job, boys!" he yells in crossing.

"Nicely done, boys," Coach congratulates us as we take our spots on the bench. "Just keep doing that all day."

He gives us each a fist bump as we settle in for the defense taking the field.

The fans are amped up, cheering us on.

But the game isn't a giveaway. Chicago answers with a touchdown of their own.

Back and forth it goes all afternoon. Chicago takes the lead by a field goal before the half, but our defense is ready for them in the third quarter. They're playing lights out. Every player, every line showed up for the game today.

And it shows.

When the final whistle blows, we come out on top, 27-24.

The locker room is raucous. Music is pumping from someone's locker as we celebrate the win.

"That was a good team win. I want you all to enjoy tonight and tomorrow, and we'll look at what we can clean up next week." Coach's words are barely audible over the noise.

Nothing like starting the season 1-0.

After talking to the press and answering questions about the game—thankfully no questions about my recent exploits—I take a quick shower and head out.

Where I find Peyton waiting for me.

"What are you doing down here?"

Her smile does more to me than any touchdown ever could.

"Still had my pass." She flashes the badge hanging around her neck. "Thought I'd come down and see you."

"Pretty good first game."

Peyton shrugs her shoulder. "One hundred and two yards. Not bad."

"Not bad, huh? Also had two touchdowns."

I close the small distance between us.

"Maybe next time you should try for three." Peyton gives me a playful smile.

"Always so hard to impress, Rocky."

"Maybe when I see something that impresses me, I'll be impressed."

I bark out a laugh. "I'll try for three touchdowns next time."

"Then I'll be impressed." Peyton pushes off the wall. "I should get going. We have the adoption event this week, and I want to make sure we're all set."

I nod. Peyton easily slips back to all business. "Right."

"You're heading straight home, correct?"

I try not to wince at her words, but she's said them for obvious reasons. "Early night for me. I'll head home and watch some of the late games and go to bed at a decent hour."

"Good."

We're facing each other, neither one of us moving or knowing what to do next. I start to move, just as she does. We're dancing around each other.

Pretty apt description for how we've been lately.

Smiling at Peyton, I move around her.

"I guess I'll see you tomorrow?" I spin on my heel, ready to head home and relax after the win.

"I forgot how much I loved it." Peyton draws me back.

Turning back, I quirk a brow at her. "Loved what?"

"Watching you play."

Her words wash over me and settle into a part of me that I forgot was there. The part that belonged to her. That has always belonged to her.

And if I'm not careful, I'll lose my heart to her again.

"Night, Peyton."

Chapter Fifteen

PEYTON

"Peyton. Thanks so much for being here today. We're really excited to have Colin help us get these dogs adopted." Nicole, the director of the Lab rescue in Denver, shakes my hand.

"He's been excited all week."

The man in question is sitting on the ground being swarmed by dogs. Each and every one is trying to lick his face and get pets from him. And Colin is eating up every ounce of attention. I know it's going to go a long way in getting a lot of these dogs adopted today.

"You said you wanted to do a photo op before we get started?"

I nod. "Yes. Hopefully it'll help bring in more crowds today."

A few of the dogs are just sitting within the temporary fence that was constructed for the event at City Park. It breaks my heart that they're all here today, but I'm hoping Colin helps make this event a success. I don't tell him that I handpicked it for a reason.

"Which dogs do you want me with?" Colin's smile is dazzling in the early afternoon sunshine.

"How about this one?" I'm standing next to Waffles, the sweet yellow Lab puppy. He hasn't gone to play with the other dogs, but has been sniffing the area around him.

"Waffles? What kind of name is that for a dog?"

Waffles turns to face Colin, almost giving him the same look I do.

"Does it really matter?"

"Find me a Pancake and I'll have my breakfast pals." Colin laughs.

"Oh God, that's terrible." I try to stifle my laugh.

"And yet, you still laughed." Colin isn't looking at me. He's picked up Waffles, the small dog licking his chin. "Hey buddy. Are you hoping to get adopted today?"

The puppy in Colin's arms is doing weird things to my insides. They're both looking at each other like they're the best thing they've seen. I snap a picture before I think too much about it.

"This will be great." I'm doing my thing on his social media since Earl didn't want him to have control over it, all the while ignoring the warm-blooded male who is now in my space.

"Aww. It looks like the little guy likes me." Colin is peering over my shoulder as I post.

"And it only took someone of the four-legged species to do it." I give Waffles an affectionate rub on the head before wandering off to document the event.

It's the perfect late-summer day for this event. The sun is hot, and the sky is clear, drawing lots of people to the park.

Families with young kids are running around playing with the dogs. A few have come up to congratulate Colin on the win this past weekend.

He's carefree and affectionate with his attention. He takes some of the dogs that aren't playing with others and introduces them to some of the families.

Colin has the magic touch.

This is the Colin I remember. The one from college who was so giving with his love and attention. Not the playboy he became after joining the league.

It's like Colin knows I'm thinking about him and his eyes find mine.

His dimples pop as he gives me a smile.

My insides turn to complete mush at the sight. It's a feeling that's long been asleep inside me. No one but Colin could ever make me feel like this. All it took was one smile from him to realize that he's slowly been chipping away at the walls around my heart.

I wish I could blame the heat in my cheeks on the sun. But it's because of the man staring back at me.

Colin

IT'S BEEN AN EXHAUSTING AFTERNOON. Out of the seventeen dogs that were brought today, fifteen were adopted. One is still too young but is with the rescue's director, and then there's my guy, Waffles, who has been following me around all day, and I can't say that I mind.

"Seems you've got a fan there." Nicole motions next to me. "He doesn't warm up to a lot of people."

"I guess we speak the same language." I get down on Waffles's level, petting his head. He leans in to chew on my watch.

"Any chance you want to take him home with you?"

"Me?" I sit on the ground, and Waffles crawls into my lap. "I've never had a dog of my own. And my schedule is too crazy with traveling to away games."

Nicole rolls her eyes at me as Peyton strolls over to us. "Peyton, tell Colin he should adopt Waffles."

"Waffles didn't get adopted?"

The hurt look in Peyton's eyes is evident. It has me answering before I can think twice. "I'm adopting him."

"You will?" Nicole sounds so excited, and I can only nod in agreement.

"I mean, I'm sure there's a process to make sure I'm a good owner." I flash my pearly whites at her.

"If Peyton here will vouch for you, that's good enough for me."

"What do you say, Rocky? You wouldn't make this poor guy go back to sleeping on the floor, would you?"

"You do know where dogs sleep, right?" She looks at me like I'm an idiot.

"Waffles is sleeping with me. Only the best for my guy." As if he knows I need help, he barks in agreement. "See? He likes me."

"I'll vouch for you. Only because I'll hurt you if he's not treated like a king."

"Waffles, I think this is the beginning of a beautiful friendship." I kiss his soft fur and set him back in my lap.

"Great! I'll go get the paperwork. He's got an appointment tomorrow, so I can bring him to you after we finish." Nicole gives Peyton a hug and is off to finish cleaning up.

"You want to go out tonight and celebrate?" I ask.

"Don't you need to go and get stuff for Waffles?" Peyton leans over, scratching him on the ears.

"I can do that tomorrow. I'm a dog dad now. Can't be going out all the time now with this little guy."

"You know just when to flash that dimple, don't you?" Peyton asks, hiding her own smile.

"What can I say? It got me you."

Chapter Sixteen

COLIN

It didn't take much to get Peyton to come out with me. Not when I lured her with the promise of Mexican food.

My girl is a sucker for chips and guacamole.

And I used that to my advantage.

"Have you ever been here?" I ask, holding the door open for her.

It is a tiny dive bar, tucked into my old neighborhood from before I moved somewhere more private.

"I haven't. Most of my time is spent out in Boulder. Well, it was spent in Boulder."

Placing a hand on her back, I guide us toward the bar.

"Colin! Long time no see." The bartender waves us over to a pair of empty stools.

"Hey man, good to see you." I pull Rodrigo, the owner, in for a hug. I got to know him well since I came here a lot to decompress. He always liked being behind the bar, talking with people and getting to know them.

"Where've you been?" He grabs my usual, Pacifico, and drops two in front of us. "Great game last week.

Denver's going to be hard to beat if you keep playing like that."

"Glad all that practice pays off." I slide one of the beers over to Peyton. "Can we get some guac whenever you get a minute?"

"Sure thing. I'll give you and your lady friend some time before ordering." He winks at Peyton before going over to other patrons.

"Do you bring all your lady friends here, Colin?" Peyton rolls her eyes as she takes a long pull of her beer. I'm entranced by the way her lips wrap around the top of the bottle. It doesn't take a lot of imagination to imagine those lips wrapped around something else.

Fuck. I shift in my seat, trying to quell the desire now running through me.

"Is that how you see me, Rocky? As just some massive playboy?" The ice-cold beer soothes the heat in my veins. The last thing I want to do is scare Peyton off. She's only just warming up to me, and I don't want to send her in the other direction.

"Would I be here if you were a saint?" She leans back, crossing one leg over the other.

"Touché," I laugh. "But there has to be some hope for me."

Peyton's eyes skate over every inch of me. My skin feels too tight for my body.

I've changed since college. The Colin she knew then isn't the same one she knows now. My walls went up to keep people out. Because I couldn't afford to lose my heart to anyone. Not like I did to her.

"You did well today." She's quiet as she sips her beer. The neon lights from the bar cast her in an almost-ethereal glow.

"How much did it pain you to say that?"

Rodrigo drops off a basket of chips and guac in front of us.

"Thanks, man."

I nod to him as Peyton grabs a chip and dunks it in the bowl. "You don't need me to pump up your ego, but all the comments on social media have been positive so far."

"As long as the team is taking notice."

"They are. They loved the footage from today. Fans want to see you with Waffles once you bring him home."

A smile hits me hard thinking about the little ball of fur. "I can't wait to bring him home. What if he doesn't like my house? Or I get him the wrong food? Shit, is there a wrong food?"

Peyton drops a warm hand on my arm. "Waffles wouldn't leave your side today. I don't think you have anything to worry about."

"Will you be there when Nicole brings him home?"

"I think you can manage. Waffles is a puppy. You'll do great." She sinks another chip into the thick dip. "I don't think you need me there to post about it on social media."

"Peyton." I grab her wrist. "I don't want you there because it'd be good for my reputation. I just want you there for me."

The words slip out before I have a chance to pull them back in. It'd be so much easier to pass this off as needing her to help fix me in the eyes of the public. But ever since she walked into that conference room, I've wanted to be the man she knows I can be. Someone deserving of her.

"When did you change?"

"What?" Her question catches me off guard.

"This"—she waves her hand in front of me after setting down the loaded chip— "is the you I know. When did you change?"

"They day I got drafted by Denver."

Peyton narrows her eyes at me. "You had that ready to go."

"It's the truth."

"And what, you just fell into the playboy image you put out there for everyone to see?"

"Easier than putting my heart on the line." Peyton was the only person to ever bring out the honesty in me. These past few years it was easier to hide behind the image of how I was perceived than to show my true self. The man who only wanted one person.

Peyton.

Needing something to do, I grab her chip and take a bite out of it.

"Hey! That was mine!" She grabs me before I can finish it and closes her mouth around my fingers to take the last of it.

Shit. Her lips, wrapped around my fingers, are not good for my self-control. The way her eyes widen tells me she feels this too.

This whole conversation we've been having is stirring up all sorts of emotions. Ones that I thought I had locked down.

"Ready to order?" Rodrigo breaks the stare down between the two of us as I order both of us the signature tacos.

"Ballsy of you to assume I'd like the tacos." Peyton chomps down onto her chip, giving me a playful look.

"Do you not like tacos anymore?"

Peyton rolls her eyes at me. This. This is easy between us. Keeping it light. "If I ever decline tacos, you know something is wrong with me."

"Good to know."

The rest of the night passes easily—conversation light

and flowing. By the time we're getting up to leave, I want to yank her back down and keep her here.

I'm just not ready for the night to end.

I twirl my keys in my hand as I walk Peyton to her car. "What time do you want me to pick you up tomorrow?"

"Just text me when you're up." She smiles at me.

Peyton goes to open her car door, but I grab it, stopping her. "How about a goodbye hug?"

"Only because you did a great job today."

Holding out my arms, Peyton steps into them.

The moment her hands connect with my waist and hold on, something clicks into place. A deep sigh escapes as I rest my head on the crown of hers.

Heat flares inside of me where every inch of Peyton presses against me.

Should I be worried someone could snap our picture and ruin any progress I've made? Sure. But not in my old neighborhood. People here couldn't care less about having me around.

Peyton's fingers tighten, tiny little brands where they meet me. I can feel the heat through my thin T-shirt.

We fit together like two pieces of a puzzle.

When she pulls back, cold swoops in.

"I'll see you tomorrow." She climbs into her car, and I watch her drive off.

The thought of spending another day with her tomorrow has a smile stretching across my face.

It feels like I finally have Peyton back. And maybe, just maybe, something could work between the two of us.

Chapter Seventeen

PEYTON

"Colin. You don't need any more toys."

"But what if he doesn't like the dinosaur?" Colin throws two rope toys into the cart as we meander through the aisles at the pet store.

When he asked me to be there with him when Nicole brought Waffles home, I didn't think it included a trip to the store.

"Waffles will be happy he doesn't have to share his toys with anyone."

"How many other dogs was he with?" Colin guides the cart around the corner. We've garnered a few glances here and there, but no one has stopped to ask for a photo.

"Nicole has three fosters right now." I stop to grab a bag of bones for Waffles.

"I can't believe anyone wouldn't want him. I'm going to give him the best life."

Colin's brows are pulled tight in concentration. My heart tugs inside my chest at how caring he's being right now. It's been flopping around ever since I left him last night with that lingering hug.

How can a hug be charged?

I felt it in every part of me. Parts of me that needed relief after.

I shake my head, not needing to think about that.

"Peyton, look how cute this is!" Colin looks like a kid at Christmas as he holds up the tiny football. "Can we get it?"

I laugh. "Would you listen to me if I said no?"

"Probably not." He throws it into the cart as we finish getting the last few things he needs.

"I'm going to do okay at this, right?" Colin is nervous. It's not something I'm used to as we check out and load everything into the back of his truck.

"You'll do just fine, I promise. Dogs are easy. And Waffles already likes you."

"God, it's worse than reading to the kids!"

"And how did that turn out for you?"

"Fine, I guess," Colin grumbles.

"See? You're going to do great."

Colin makes the quick drive home to his house in one of the nicer communities in Cherry Creek.

There's a car waiting in front of his house when we pull up.

"Sorry. I know I'm early, but I had to take one of the other pups to the vet this morning." Nicole rushes out as soon as we get out of the car.

Waffles hops out and starts sniffing around.

"This is your new home, Waffles!" Colin opens the gate to let him into his front yard. The dog in question sniffs his way up the sidewalk as Colin is watching him. I can feel his nerves from where I'm standing.

"Relax, Colin. It's going to be okay." I give him a reassuring smile.

I don't think I've ever seen him this nervous. Waffles

snoops around the garden beds before coming to sit in front of Colin. His tiny head cocks to one side.

"Hey, buddy. I'm going to be your new dad." Colin squats in front of him, holding the football toy in one hand and his other hand out for Waffles to sniff.

Waffles sticks his nose in Colin's hand, then leaps into his arms. They both fall to the ground as the wiggling pups showers his face with kisses.

"That's right. I'm going to be your best friend." Colin's voice raises an octave as he snuggles the dog in his arms.

There go the rest of my insides. Completely melting for the guy squeaking a football dog toy.

"I think Waffles is going to do just fine here." Nicole nudges my shoulder before quietly sneaking out the front gate. She doesn't make a big fuss about saying goodbye, allowing this new family to bond.

Colin

"I SHOULD PROBABLY GET GOING." Peyton moves off the couch. Waffles snuggles in deeper to the space she just left. She's completely won him over.

My dog has good taste.

"Stay. Let me order us dinner."

Peyton goes to grab her jacket from the kitchen. "I need to get going anyway. It'll be a long drive home tonight."

"You can stay here. I have plenty of room," I hear myself offering.

"I don't think that's a good idea." Peyton shrugs into her coat, leaning back against the kitchen bar.

"I've had worse ideas. C'mon, you know you want to." I take a hesitant step closer to her. "We can talk."

"About what?"

"Don't you want to know about how I've been doing?"

Peyton rolls her eyes at me. "I know how you've been doing. I need to get going."

I'm racking my brain, trying to find a reason for her to stay. I didn't realize how much I wanted it until she's getting ready to leave. I like having her here in my space.

"Don't you want to know how I've been playing?" I'm reaching, I know it. But I don't care.

"Talk to me when you've had a two-thousand-yard season," Peyton whispers, but not quietly enough.

That's it.

I close the distance between us, caging her in, her back to my front.

"What was that? I couldn't quite hear you." Brushing her hair to the side, I whisper the words again, my breath ghosting her neck. Goose bumps appear on her skin. "What'd you say?"

"It's not like you had a two-thousand-yard season," she says on a sigh.

"And how would you know that?" I press into her, letting her feel every hard inch of me. And I mean every hard inch.

"I might have watched a game or two."

"Or two." I fight to hold in the laugh, but now that I know, I prod her. "How many did you watch, Rocky?"

She spins in my arms, crossing her own to act as a shield. "Fine, all of them. Is that what you wanted to hear?"

I can't help the grin that slides across my face.

"You don't have to look so smug. It's not a good look for you."

"I'm just picturing you wearing my jersey and watching all of my games."

"No one said I wore your jersey."

I lean closer, inhaling her sweet scent. "In my fantasy, you are."

"God, Colin."

I get even closer, wedging a knee between her legs. "So tell me, how did I measure up to Peyton's standards?"

"You were okay."

"Just okay?" I raise a brow at her. My rookie season was more than okay. If it weren't for the standout quarterback on Indianapolis's team, I would've gotten rookie of the year.

"Only six touchdowns. I know you could've done better." Her tone is icy, but I see the smile she is fighting.

"Ouch."

"Average of nine-point-eight yards per reception? What, Colin, you couldn't get that extra half foot to make it to ten?"

God, listening to this woman spout off my stats is better than any foreplay.

"Still led all rookies that season." I lean closer, my mouth only an inch from hers.

"At least you cracked one hundred receptions."

When Peyton's eyes drop to my lips, I don't hesitate. I take her mouth in a crushing kiss. I swallow her gasp, letting my tongue tangle with hers.

Fuck, I love kissing her.

I sink into this kiss, rolling my tongue against hers. Each touch sends lust coiling tight in my gut. I want to do a lot more than kiss her.

Her fists tighten in my shirt, as if trying to decide

whether she wants to push me away or pull me in tighter. My hands don't have the same indecision, drifting down her sides and settling on her hips.

One taste and I'm hooked. Like the worst addict, I know one hit of Peyton's lips won't be enough. It will never be enough.

But all too soon, it's over.

"Oh God." Peyton covers her swollen lips with her fingers, using the other hand to push me back. "I have to go."

Spinning on her heel, she's gone in the blink of an eye.

Peyton might be running scared, but that kiss?

Fuck me, that kiss just reminded me of everything I had wanted in my life at one time.

Peyton.

Only Peyton.

Chapter Eighteen

COLIN

"How does it feel to be back playing against LA, Jackson?" Alex watches another defensive play on the iPad in his hand.

"As long as they don't come at me, I'll be fine." I don't miss the anger in his eyes.

"If they do, they'll have me to mess with," Knox snarls. The cracking of his knuckles tells me he means business.

"You better not do anything to get yourself thrown out of the game," Alex states matter-of-factly. Even though we're all captains, he's the leader of this team, and we all look to him for guidance. "This is going to be a hard-fought game."

"Alex, we're ready. You know there is such a thing as overpreparing, right?" I tell him.

Alex slaps the case of his iPad closed and looks at me. "Alright. How about we talk about you then?"

"Why do you want to talk about me?" I fiddle with the cap of my water bottle.

"The last time we talked, I believe you were trying to get back into someone's good graces."

Shit. "This isn't something we need to talk about."

A wily smile spreads across his face. "Oh, I think we do. From what I've seen, there has been no mention of you in any tabloids lately. Seems like you're on the up and up again."

"From what Tenley tells me, she couldn't take her eyes off you." Jackson waggles his eyebrows at me.

"Wait, you know who this is?" Alex slaps his chest. "Why have you been holding out on us?"

Jackson shrugs. "I figured it was common knowledge."

Knox rolls his eyes. "You wouldn't know unless Tenley pointed it out. Otherwise, I doubt you would've seen past her."

A happy look washes over his face.

"Do I look like that when I talk about her?" I point to Jackson.

Alex nods. "Plain as day. Jackson just doesn't notice because he's happy."

He leans back in his chair, crossing his arms. "I highly recommend it."

"Back to the girl." Alex waves him off. "It's Peyton, right?"

"Shh." I quiet him down, even though we're the only four in the room. What started as a captains' meeting has quickly devolved into a meeting on my love life. "We're not technically allowed to be together. I mean, I wouldn't even consider us together at this point."

"Ahh, fuck," Knox whispers. The twisted look on his face tells me there's more to his words than he's letting on.

"Let me ask you this. Is she worth you jeopardizing your career?" Alex's voice is firm. I don't miss the hard look in his eyes.

I hesitate. For the very first time, I stop and think about what we're doing. I didn't think twice after that kiss we shared. It was all the pent-up frustration we felt and the years apart boiling out of us into one hot-as-fuck kiss.

A kiss shouldn't be that hot. But damn was it ever.

"It's not *my* career I'm worried about."

"That wasn't my question." Alex rests his arms on the table. "It's not just her career on the line. What happens if you get traded? What happens to all of us?"

I look around at the faces staring back at me. "Do you not think I've thought about that? Fuck, some days it's all I think about. I know my past actions have reflected poorly on the team—"

Knox snorts. "That's one way of putting it."

I flip him off. "But I'm trying, okay? I want to be with her. It just makes sense to me."

Jackson clasps me on the shoulder. "Then be careful. We love you, Colin, and we don't want anything happening to you."

I wipe a fake tear away, dissolving the growing tension in the room. "Aww, would you look at that. The grump has a heart of gold."

"Fuck off, man."

"Happy looks good on you. I'm serious."

Jackson was one grumpy son of a bitch last year with his knee problems. Turns out, all he needed was Tenley to turn him around.

Am I like Jackson? Except the guys only see me as a playboy with no commitment to anything? But I don't want to keep going through life like that.

That one kiss with Peyton brought me to my knees. I want to worship her like I know she deserves. But the question remains—is she ready for more?

"I can't with you guys," Knox say as he laughs. "You guys are worse than my grandma and her friends."

"I will attest to that. Don't get on their bad side." I

cringe. "I don't think I knew bingo could ever get so heated."

Knox points at me. "And they play for lottery tickets. Don't get between them and their scratchers."

"Knox! I need to go over a few new schemes with you. Meet me in the conference room in ten." Frankie pops her head into one of the rooms we've commandeered before popping right out.

"Jesus. How many times do we have to look at their offense?" He glugs back the rest of his water and gets up.

"What'd you do to get on her bad side?" I ask.

Knox cracks his neck as he starts backing out of the room. "Fuck if I know."

"Go. Learn the offense so you can sack the quarterback like we all know you can." I give Knox my best smile.

Knox gives me a saccharine smile back. "And go learn the passing routes so you can catch the ball and not get picked off."

"Hey! That's a dig at me," Alex pipes up. "Get the fuck outta here and don't piss off your coach."

Knox gives him a mock salute on the way out. "Yes, captain."

I can't help but laugh. These guys are more like my family than my actual family. And I would do anything to spend my entire career playing by their sides.

But does that include putting my personal life on hold? On not seeing if this thing with Peyton could become more?

At one point, she was the only future I wanted.

Is this something I can wish for in the future?

One can only hope.

Chapter Nineteen

PEYTON

It's late. I probably shouldn't be here, but I am. There are a few events coming up this week for Colin, and I want to discuss them with him before he retreats into himself.

The game against LA was hard-fought, but Denver came out on the losing end, 24-21. Nothing like losing on a last minute field goal.

Anxiety ripples through me. I haven't been back to Colin's house since he kissed me. I didn't want to be alone with him. I was worried I'd want a repeat. And that a repeat would lead to more.

"Peyton, what are you doing here?" Colin looks exhausted when he answers the door. Waffles is right at his feet, tail wagging.

"We didn't get a chance to go over your schedule for the week."

"Can't this wait until tomorrow?"

"No. Earl has a benefit dinner for you tomorrow, so we need to go over it now."

"Fuck me." He swings the door open farther and beckons me in. "C'mon, Waffles."

I follow him into the kitchen, his shoulders slumped in defeat.

"Can you make it fast?" Colin falls onto a barstool, his eyes urging me on.

"It wasn't your fault today, you know." I set my purse down on the counter in front of me. It feels like an island between us at his stiff posture.

"I didn't play my best. How isn't it my fault?" he gripes. "I've already heard from my dad about it. Needing to play better."

Athletes. They're all the same. Taking the blame when it didn't come down to one person.

"You were in bounds on that last catch when the refs ruled you out and didn't overturn it. There's nothing you could've done about it."

"Just like I couldn't have done anything about a lot of things," Colin whispers.

"What?" My ears perk up at his words.

"You say it's not my fault, but it seems like a lot of things are actually my fault."

"What does this have to do with the game today?"

He shakes his head. Colin stands, a full head taller than me. "It has to do with us. I'm sick of beating around the bush."

Colin is giving me whiplash with this conversation. "I came to talk about your schedule this week. How did we end up talking about us?"

"I want to talk about us. You never seem to want to." Colin turns his back on me. The tension coming off him is palpable.

"You want to talk about us? Fine." I don't know why

this man has the power to infuriate me in a single breath. But he does. "Tell me why you left."

He spins on his heel, his face deadly serious. "Why *I* left? Why *you* left!"

"You pushed me away like I meant nothing to you!" There's no stopping the anger that comes out. "You were everything to me, Colin! And you treated me like I was nothing."

"Me? What about you? You were the one who wrote me a 'Dear John' letter. That was it."

"What the hell are you talking about?"

"You sent me a letter. Told me that things got too intense after our scare and you couldn't handle it. You wished me luck in the draft and told me not to contact you." His chest heaves with each breath he takes.

"I never sent you a letter. You sent me one."

"No, I didn't."

I shake my head. "You did. And you tore my heart out."

"No, I didn't." Colin is adamant. "You sent me one."

"This conversation isn't getting us anywhere." I go to grab my bag, but Colin stops me.

"Don't walk away from me, Peyton. Not again. Not this time."

The power radiating off him stops me.

The air crackles. It's a lightning storm ready to ignite. One spark and we'll combust. Colin takes a step toward me. The heat in his eyes is undeniable.

Another step.

He's so close I can see the gleam in his eyes. It was always there, right before he made his move. Five years later and he still has it.

It sets off a firestorm in my core. I want to hate that Colin still makes me feel like this. That he's the only man to make me feel like this, but I can't. Not when he's looking at me like he wants to devour me.

His brow quirks up in the slightest move, as if asking if it's okay. My only response is to crush my body to his.

Nothing has ever felt so right as his lips against mine. Colin dominates this kiss. I forgot how his kisses made me feel. How good it felt to feel his tongue against mine.

A whimper escapes my lips that he easily swallows. His tongue tangles with mine. It sends an inferno sweeping through my body, gathering in my core.

"Fuck, Peyton." Colin leans back, his hands caressing my face. "Fuck."

His breath is hot on my face. The low lights of his living room cast him in an ethereal glow. I had pushed out of my mind how sexy he is.

But this Colin is different from the one I knew in college.

His shoulders are broader. His biceps grew in size. I rest a hand on his stomach, only imagining what the hard muscles underneath look like. This is my Colin and not my Colin all rolled into one man.

The one man I said I wasn't going to let take me again.

But here we are.

"Where'd you go?" Colin dips his mouth closer to mine. His tongue traces my lower lip.

"Just thinking about how much I want you." I don't hide the need in my voice.

Colin lifts me into his arms with ease. I tangle my fingers in the soft strands of his hair as he drinks me in with this kiss. It's softer, but no less passionate. I cling to him, as if he might disappear if I don't hold on tight enough.

He carries me through the house to his room, closing the door so no four-legged friends come bounding in.

Setting one knee on the bed, Colin lays me out before him. His erection is obvious in his workout shorts.

As much as this is about reconnecting, I also need to feel him everywhere. Grabbing the hem of my shirt, I pull it off and throw it behind me.

"No one ever measured up to you," he murmured.

"What?"

Colin drags a finger down the center of my chest, between the valley of my breasts. Goose bumps erupt in his wake as he traces the waistband of my pants.

"No matter what I did, no one could ever replace you." His whispered words unlock the part of my heart that I closed off to love. To everyone that wasn't him.

The sheer pain in his eyes has the ice melting around my heart. Fisting his shirt in my hands, I pull him down to me. I pour everything I'm feeling into this kiss. I cling to him, not wanting to lose a moment with him.

Because in the dark recesses of my mind, I know this shouldn't be happening. Earl was very clear that fraternizing at work was not allowed. But it's hard to care about that when Colin settles his weight over me. I'm aching to feel him skin to skin.

"Colin," I beg. "I need to feel you."

I'm not prepared for the sight before me when Colin pulls his shirt off. He has too many abs to count. His pecs could be islands, they're so defined. A light smattering of hair covers him; that hasn't changed.

"Like what you see?"

I lick my lips. "I think you know that."

"Christ. I still can't believe you're here." His whispered words wash over me. It's hard to believe I really am here.

"I used to dream about this. That we'd find each other again."

"Oh yeah? What'd you dream about?" Colin lays a

warm hand on my stomach. The butterflies in my stomach fight to be the closest one to his touch.

"Something pretty similar to this. Except your mouth was on me."

Colin smirks. "I think I can arrange that."

His fingers dip below the waistband of my pants, setting off a new round of fireworks as his mouth licks a trail up my stomach.

"I forgot how much I liked your tits." My eyes track his as his tongue traces the cups of my satin bra. "Perfect size for my hands. Always so responsive."

Colin pulls the cup of my bra down, exposing my already hard nipple. His tongue flicks it ever so softly, but I feel it everywhere. My back arches off the bed, needing more of him.

"More," I whine.

"More what?" Colin's other hand works the button of my pants open and drags the zipper down.

"Everything. I just need you."

I'm exposing myself more than I want to with those words, but I'm too far gone to care.

Because this is Colin.

My Colin.

He was once my everything.

And now that I have him again, I don't want to waste a minute.

"Your wish is my command, Rocky."

Colin's teeth close around my nipple and a moan bursts free. The attention he's giving me is unmatched. He knows exactly what I need without me telling him.

As his tongue crosses to my other breast, his fingers brush over the thin material covering my pussy.

"Someone's already wet for me." I wrap a leg around him, trying to draw him in closer.

A garbled response is the best I can do as he sweeps the scrap of lace to the side and plunges a finger into my tight channel.

"Are you going to come like this?" Colin is needy as he tongues my nipple while thrusting a single finger in and out of me.

"Don't stop!" My nails dig into his back as I cling to the last strings of my sanity before he rips my world wide open. There's no going back after this. But I don't want to.

Colin curls his finger inside me as he sucks on my nipple. I'm so worked up, the combination sends me spiraling into a world of stars and colors. Every nerve is alight as Colin steers me through one of the most intense orgasms I can ever remember having.

By the time he's pulling his finger out of me, I'm floating on air. His weight on top of me is the only thing keeping me grounded.

"I forgot how beautiful you are when you come." Colin sucks on the pulse in my neck.

An easy smile crosses my face as I relish the feeling of his lips on me. "It's just how I remember."

"Oh yeah?" Colin pops up, resting his hands on either side of my head. His lips are wet and swollen from kisses.

"Mmm, yes. But I wonder." Placing one hand in the center of his well-defined chest, I push him back onto the bed.

"Yes?" Colin asks.

"Do you still look the same when you come?"

Standing, I shed the last of my clothes and crawl into his lap.

"It's a theory I'd love to test." Colin nips at my jaw, threading his hand through my hair to give him a better angle.

His warm lips on me are turning me to goo. His hands

touching my skin are setting me on fire. I'm feeling too much but not enough with Colin.

Trailing one hand down his chest, I dip into the waist-band of his shorts to find velvet steel waiting for me.

"Still going commando, I see."

"No sense doing otherwise when I'm just hanging out around the house."

I give him a hard stroke, loving how he fits in my hand. His tip glistens as I work him over. Colin's head is thrown back in pleasure. I love seeing what I do to him.

"Fuck. You're so damn good at this."

Colin thrusts up into my hand, smearing more precum as he goes.

"Fuck, Peyton. So good, but I don't think I can last."

He pulls my hand off of him and the intensity in his eyes could send me flying.

"I want you inside me." I wrap my arms around his neck, dropping my forehead to his.

Adjusting, Colin pushes his shorts down and reaches over to the nightstand to pull out a condom packet. My eyes follow his hands as he rolls it down his shaft. It's an angry red. And I can't wait to feel it inside me. Stretching me and hitting a spot so deep, that only Colin was ever able to do it.

Pushing up onto my knees, I hold my breath as Colin lines himself up with me and I sink down onto him.

"Holy shit," I breathe. Colin was always big, but I forgot how he used to stretch me and fill me. It sucks the breath from me.

Colin's fingers find my clit and dance over it to ease the sting. "You okay, Rocky?"

I nod as I sink down farther. His featherlight touch distracts me from the bite of pain as I take him fully inside me.

"I forgot how big you are."

Colin grabs my chin with his free hand, pulling me down to him. "Something I never mind hearing."

And then his lips are on me in a bruising kiss. It's hard to contain everything I'm feeling as I start moving over him, matching my moves to his.

It's easy, the give and take we share. It's like our bodies were made for one another and no one else.

My hands are all over him, seeking purchase anywhere I can find.

"Oh God, Colin. I'm so close."

"I'm there." His breath is hot against my neck as I barrel toward my second orgasm of the night. A swivel of my hips, Colin's deft fingers on my clit, and I'm coming undone around him. Strong hands hold me as he continues thrusting into me. The vibrations against my skin tells me he's coming too.

Feeling Colin pulse inside me, how he strung me out and drew every last ounce of pleasure from me, is something only he knows how to do.

We're quiet as we come down from our highs.

"Damn, Peyton. I forgot how good that feels."

"Me too." I sink my hands into his hair, holding him close to me.

Because this feeling of being close to him?

I want to hold on with both hands and never let go.

Chapter Twenty

PEYTON

Scratching at the door pulls me awake. A heavy arm is draped over my stomach, keeping me locked tight to him. I bury my smile in the pillow, loving waking up in Colin's arms.

But the scratching at the door doesn't stop. Glancing at the clock, I realize it's already seven. Thankfully, my internship allows me the flexibility to not be in the office. Especially when I'm working with the guy currently in bed with me.

Grabbing Colin's T-shirt from the end of the bed, I sneak across the room. The second I open the door, Waffles greets me with an excited yip.

"Hi, buddy. Sorry you didn't get to sleep with your dad last night." I pick him up, burying my face in his soft fur. There's nothing better than the smell of a puppy.

I carry him down the stairs and am greeted with an explosion of stuffing.

"Holy shit."

Waffles wiggles in my arms, ready to go play in the chaos that is now Colin's living room.

"What'd you do?" Waffles runs over to the couch, hopping onto the back. His tail is wagging behind him, like he's proud of what he did.

"What the hell?" Colin booms behind me. Waffles barks at him before running over. "What'd you do, buddy?"

Colin tries to sound scolding, but he can't. He's already wrapped around Waffles's little paw.

"I'm guessing he was mad he didn't get to sleep in his usual spot."

Colin wraps an arm around me, pulling me into him. His skin is still warm from sleep. "He might have to get used to it." Colin nibbles on my neck.

"We'll have to train him then."

I spin in Colin's arms. His hair is mussed from my hands being in it all night. We didn't just stop at one. It's like we were making up for lost time and had to try and cram in as many orgasms as possible.

Not that I minded, even if I am a little sore this morning.

"What's this *we* I'm hearing?"

My hands drift up his pecs, linking around his neck. I pull him down closer to me. His breath is minty fresh.

"I'm only assuming you're going to need help with the little guy while you're out of town."

Colin looks down at Waffles now sitting at our feet.

"You think you can be good for her? Not scare her off?" Waffles just stares up at Colin.

"I think he needs to eat and go out."

Colin takes Waffles outside, opening the door for him so he can come in when he's done. While he gets his food out, I start the coffee.

I hop up on the counter while the coffee brews and watch as Waffles bounds in to meet Colin.

It's easy to see how much these two love each other. I'm not sure who has bigger puppy eyes looking at the other, Colin or Waffles.

"What's that face for?" Colin's voice pulls me back to present.

"Just enjoying the morning sights."

"Oh yeah?" Colin steps between my legs, pushing them apart. His hands stay locked on my knees.

"My guys look pretty cute together."

"Oh, so we're your guys now?"

I shrug my shoulder. "I mean, if you want to be."

Heat flares in Colin's eyes. "There's only one answer to that question."

"Good." I lean forward, capturing Colin's lips with mine. His morning stubble scratches my chin.

"Do you have work to do today?" Colin rests his forehead against mine. His fingers drift higher, playing with the hem of his shirt.

"You're the job." The words are out of my mouth before I can think twice about them. It's a sobering thought. Earl is clear—no fraternizing at work.

"Where'd you go?" Colin drops a kiss in the space below my ear.

"We can't be seen together." I push him back, looking into his deep blue eyes. The way his hair flops down into his face makes him look like the fresh-faced kid I met in college.

"We'll figure it out."

"I wish it were that easy."

Colin grasps my chin, locking my eyes to his. "I just got you back. Do you really think I'm going to let you go that easily?"

I smile. "I guess not."

"Good. We'll take it one day at a time. Together." I

wish I had the same confidence as Colin, but like he said, together.

"Together."

"And you know what together means, right?"

I groan. "What?"

"You're helping with living room clean-up duty."

"Waffles should have to clean up! He made the mess."

Waffles comes around the counter, licking his lips from breakfast.

"He's too cute to help clean."

"Ugh. Fine." I hop off the counter and head for the living room. Waffles tore up at least three pillows.

"Dude. Couldn't you have just slept on the couch?" Colin whispers to the dog at his feet.

"He needs to go in his crate at night." I point to the cage set up in the corner.

"But he's lonely in there," Colin whines. Picking Waffles up, he gives me his most pitiful look. "We don't want Waffles to be sad, do we?"

Propping a fist on my hip, I try to give him a stern look. "It's either he's in the crate, or you're sleeping alone."

"Sorry, buddy. Gotta take care of my girl first." He drops a kiss on his head and sets him down.

Before he sees what's coming, I smack a pillow across his chest.

"Hey! That's not fair!" Stuffing flies out of the broken pillow, fluttering down over the couch and a happy puppy.

"What? That you didn't see it coming?" I smack him again.

"Oh, it's on!" Colin grabs another one of the pillows and hits my retreating back. Feathers and stuffing are flying. Waffles is biting the air, trying to latch on to any piece he can.

I swing at Colin, but he ducks and hits me square on the ass.

Laughter bubbles out of me as we keep swinging at each other. Hit after hit, until finally we're swinging empty pillows at each other. My stomach hurts from laughing so hard.

"I think we made a bigger mess than Waffles," Colin huffs out.

The living room is complete madness. Waffles is trying to catch feathers, while others float through the air before resting on any surface it finds.

"It's all your fault." I shake my head, dropping the pillow at my feet.

"My fault?"

I nod my head. "Your dog, your fault."

A mischievous glint gleams in Colin's eyes. "In that case…"

Colin sweeps me up into his arms and goes charging upstairs. "Then some punishment must be had."

"You sound entirely too excited for that."

"You punishing me? Oh yeah."

Chapter Twenty-One

COLIN

"Feeling good today?" Alex hits my shoulder pads as I tug down the tight-fitting material of my jersey.

"Fuck yeah!" I smack him back. The energy is high in the locker room. It's always thick when we play a division rival. Vegas will be gunning for us because we're at the top of our division. "We'll make Vegas wish they never came to town."

"You got that right!" Knox leans against my locker. "I'm itching for a sack today. I'm ready to show their offensive line what playing against a real defense looks like."

"It's gonna be a good one. I know it."

Peyton's in the stands today. Earl got her a ticket to his suite since she's been doing such a great job with me. We've been spending a lot of time together, cozied up in my house. I guess it's a good thing that I shouldn't be seen out in public. Gives us more time together, just the two of us. I'm ready to impress the hell out of her today. After her little confession after the first game, I want to see that same smile on her face.

And maybe spend the night buried inside her again.

"Uh-oh. I know that look." Knox's wide eyes are looking down at me. "Is the girl here today?"

I nod. "She is."

"Guess I better throw you some passes then," Alex jokes. "Can't have you looking like a peewee player."

"No chance of that."

It was a good week at practice. No new articles about my playboy status have popped up, and the coaches were happy with the plays Alex and I were running. It's going to be a good game.

Before long, the coaches are rallying the team and we're running out of the tunnel to thunderous applause.

The fans are next level today with Vegas in town. Screams and cheers are loud as the flag is unfurled across the field for the National Anthem.

Once the singing is done, Alex and I head to midfield, ready for the coin flip. Vegas's two captains are waiting for us. They're all business, no smiles as they call tails. We win the toss and defer to the second half.

"Ready to lose?" Hollins, Vegas's star safety has a sneer on his face.

"Not today."

I extend a hand out to him, but he ignores it and jogs back to his side of the field. It shouldn't surprise me. They're one of the worst teams in the league when it comes to sportsmanship. It'll make it that much sweeter when we beat them today.

"Alright boys, let's show them whose house this is. Play clean, play smart, and let's bring this win home!" Knox shouts to the waiting defense as play kicks off.

Swigging water, I watch as Knox and the defense snuff Vegas on their first drive. Best way to start the game.

As the offense jogs out onto the field, the stadium is

silent around us. Alex commands the field. He's the conductor and we're all at his whim.

"Hook right, Forty-two break." We all clap, breaking the huddle as we line up for the pass play.

My fingers are itching to get my hands on the ball, to drive down the field. Our center hikes the ball back to Alex and everyone moves. I run down the field, cutting to the outside as the perfect spiral sails right into my open hands. Hollins is on me, pushing me out of bounds.

First down.

"I let you have that one," Hollis snarls in my face.

"As if you can stop me," I jest as I pitch the ball to the ref.

"Just you wait, James. You're not as good as you think you are."

I roll my eyes and run up to the line. Alex picks apart Vegas, easily moving into the red zone before Winchester runs it in for a touchdown.

The stands go wild as Jackson runs out to kick the point after.

"Great opening drive, boys. Few things we can clean up on the next drive, but keep playing like that, and it'll be a good game."

Coach Brooks is always positive, no matter what is happening on the field, but even if we had a perfect drive, he never wants us to get too comfortable. Things can change at the drop of a hat, so we never get complacent.

Vegas gets close, but defense holds them to a field goal.

Things settle down as we move through the game. Vegas isn't as forgiving, stopping us before we score. It doesn't stop things from getting aggressive. Our offensive line is doing everything they can to keep Alex upright, but it's been hard. The pocket has collapsed on him more than once, making him scramble.

Hollins is on me as a run play is stopped.

"Told ya you wouldn't get far." Hollins is right in my face again.

"Look at the score." I point to the sidelines. Denver 14-Vegas 10. "We're winning."

His lips curl into an unnerving smile. "Not for long, James. You better watch out."

"Fuck off, Hollins!" He's been after me all day. Chippy shots here and there. I'm ready to take a penalty to get him off my back.

Even with Hollins all over me, Alex has been moving the ball down the field. It's still anyone's game. Time is ticking down in the second quarter as we line up on third down.

Alex changes the play at the line, calling for an out route. I blow past Hollins, a smile spreading across my face as I run down the field. I turn, and the ball is coming right to me. I don't see the player lowering his head. It's the last thing I see before lights out.

Peyton

THE SICKENING CRUNCH of helmet against helmet echoes across the silent stadium. The camera cuts from the scene on the field, but I can't take my eyes off Colin's motionless body on the sidelines.

My stomach is roiling as the coaches and medical staff run to his side. Every player on the field takes a knee.

I'm helpless to do anything but watch as Colin is worked on. He's not moving.

"Can anyone get down to the locker room to check on him?" A team rep that Earl knows is in our box screaming into their phone. "We need an update on him as soon as we have one!"

"It's obvious. Hollins is a dirty player and was targeting him the whole game!"

People are shouting around me, but it's all white noise.

I try not to think about how bad this could be. Football is a rough sport, but it doesn't make it any easier watching someone go down like this.

Colin gets placed on a stretcher and is taken off the field. There's no thumbs-up to signal he's awake and okay. I don't think I've taken a breath since the hit. The crowd cheers for him as the cart disappears through the tunnel.

The ref, picking up the flag, calls the penalty. "Pass interference. Defense, number twenty-two. Ball will be placed at the spot of the foul. Automatic first down." He pauses over the noise in the stadium. "Upon further review, it has been determined that the defensive player was leading with his head. Therefore, he has been ejected from the game."

Hollins is in the ref's face, yelling about the call. The noise level erupts around the stadium as he's escorted off the field. People are screaming and booing at him as he flips everyone off as he exits.

Classy player.

"Peyton." A warm hand on my shoulder pulls my attention away from the field.

Earl's kind eyes greet me. "I want you to go with the team rep and get me an update on how Colin is doing."

"Okay," I say quietly. I can't hide my worries about Colin's injury.

"These things happen. It's all a part of the game."

"That doesn't make me worry less." The words escape before I can pull them back.

"We have the finest doctors here who will take good care of him. Now, get me an update once you know more."

Earl guides me toward the team rep, asking him to get me to Colin, and I follow him through the stadium. Pictures of the team cover the walls in the luxury suites. One of Colin scoring a touchdown catches my attention, and it has tears welling in my eyes.

Since I'm with someone from the Mountain Lions, we're taken straight down toward the offices outside the locker room. It's nothing but chaos down here as people are scrambling.

"What's going on?"

"He's being loaded into the ambulance now. They're taking him to the hospital for testing and observation."

Oh God. There is no way I can be professional right now. I want to hop in my car and meet him there.

This never happened during college. Colin took a few hits, but nothing like this. As much as I originally tried to deny him, I've been following his NFL career. It's hard not to when you love football as much as I do.

"You ready to go?" The person who I've been following turns around to address me.

"Go where?" My brain can't make heads or tails of what's going on right now.

"To the hospital. I told Earl I'd keep an eye on you, and we need to get an update."

"Oh. Sure."

Thank God for Earl.

Colin

Should everything be blurry? God, why are the lights so bright?

And what is that fucking noise? It won't shut off.

It feels like someone is banging on a drum in my head.

Whispers around me catch my attention, but it hurts too much to try to hear them. Maybe I should just go back to sleep.

Except I catch a whiff of something familiar.

Peyton?

I try to open my eyes, but it hurts just as much as before.

I succumb to the pain.

"HOW LONG IS he going to be like this?"

"It's hard to say with a brain injury."

This time, when I wake up, things are less blurry. Still fuzzy, but not as bad. The lights overhead are still too bright for me.

"When will we know?"

I know that girl. It brings a soft comfort to me, even though I have no idea what is going on or where I am.

"Once he's discharged, he'll need to follow up with the team doctors. He'll be out at least a few weeks."

A few weeks? What the fuck is going on?

"Does he have someone to watch him these first few weeks? We won't discharge him if he won't be in someone's care."

"I'll be there."

Blinking, I try to clear my vision and force the room to

come into focus. It's hazy, at best, but I see two people standing at the end of what I now see to be a hospital bed.

I don't know if they can see that my eyes are open, but when one of the people moves to my side, I know they do.

"Colin. Thank God, you're awake."

I lean into the warm hand that is now on my face. It feels nice. Right.

"Colin. How are you feeling?" I don't recognize that person.

"Like shit." My mouth is like sandpaper. A straw is brought to my lips and I suck down what little water is given to me.

"What happened?" This time, my words are clearer. It sounds more like me.

"You don't remember? Is that common?" I don't miss the blatant fear in Peyton's words.

"Very. Many concussion patients won't remember the twenty-four hours leading up to the time of concussion. With the hit he took, he likely will not remember anything from the game."

Concussion?

"Oh God, Colin."

I turn, trying to find Peyton through the blurriness, but dizziness sets in. "Fuck."

"You're going to be pretty out of it for the next few days, Mr. James. We'll keep you here and then discharge you into Ms. Thompson's care."

"Thanks."

The bed sinks next to me, and warm hands take hold of mine. I close my eyes, settling into the pleasant feeling that takes over.

"I was so scared." Fingers trace the lines on my palm. "In all the years I've been watching you play, you've never taken a hit like that."

"What happened?"

"Do you really want to know?"

I peek one eye open at Peyton. Now that she's closer, I can focus on her without straining myself.

"Shit, was it that bad?"

She nods, and this time, I notice tears dripping down her face.

"It was Hollins. He was going after you. He was ejected from the game."

"Good. That fucker deserves it."

The laugh she gives me is watery. "Glad to see you're still you."

"Were you hoping a new personality would've been knocked into me instead?"

"The hit wasn't that bad." Peyton squeezes my hand. Just being surrounded by her warmth is pulling me back under.

"God, I don't think I've ever been this tired." I close my eyes, not able to stay awake.

"The doctor said you can rest."

I murmur my agreement. "Will you be here when I wake up?"

"I'm not going anywhere."

Chapter Twenty-Two

COLIN

My head is pounding. I don't know if I've ever felt so shitty before. I ache in places I never thought would hurt before. I don't remember the hit, but from what Peyton told me, that's a good thing.

Peyton was silent on the drive home, chewing on her lip and glancing over at me any chance she got. You can almost see the waves of anxiety rippling off her as she helps me out of the car.

"You need to relax, Rocky."

Parking the car, she turns fierce brown eyes on me. "When I no longer need to stay with you to make sure you're okay, maybe then I'll relax."

The slight shake to her words tells me there will be no relaxing anytime soon. Her eyes dip down, trying to hide the emotions I know she's feeling.

"Look at me." I put as much strength into my voice as possible. I'm exhausted, and I'd rather be horizontal right now.

Tucking a finger under her chin, I bring her gaze back to mine. "The doctor wouldn't have released me if I wasn't going to be okay. Concussion protocol means I won't go back to practice before I'm fully ready. I promise you, I'm okay."

I kiss her lips softly, trying to put everything I'm feeling into comforting her.

There's nothing heated about this kiss, but it's one of the most intimate we've ever shared. I don't know how I went without her kisses for so long. For the first time in a long time, I'm finally able to breathe. Like she pushed new life into me.

"Let's get you inside." This time, when she does look at me, she gives me a soft smile.

Wrapping an arm around my waist, Peyton steers me inside. Instead of Waffles being at the door to greet me with love and affection, it's someone harsh and judgmental.

"Dad. What are you doing here?" I really should take him off the approved guest list.

He adjusts the cuffs of his shirt. "Am I not allowed to see my son after he was in the hospital?"

I scoff at his words. "And who did you have to call to figure out that I was coming home today?"

"It's been all over the news. Seems that was the only way I could be informed of your condition."

"As you can see, I'm fine."

Peyton tenses at my side.

"And who is this person you found to take care of you?" His gaze shifts from me to Peyton. "No doubt he's paid you quite a sum of money to be his nursemaid, but you can leave."

"Oh fuck me," I mutter. This is the last thing I need. The tension in my head tightens, threatening to explode. "Dad. You remember Peyton, right?"

A flash of recognition crosses his face. I don't miss the

grinding of his jaw or the narrowing of his eyes.

"Miss Thompson. How could I forget."

"It's nice to see you, Mr. James." Peyton's words are polite, but I don't miss the underlying iciness to them.

"I can take over from here. Your services are no longer needed."

"Dad."

"You're clearly not in a position to think straight, so I will be able to assist you with anything you might need."

For fuck's sake. "Dad, I don't need your help. Peyton has everything under control."

"I can leave if you want me to."

She starts to pull back, but I pull her in closer. "No." I turn my gaze back to my dad. "Peyton's presence is needed. Yours is not. I'll text you if things change, but until then, you can leave."

He stalks toward me. "I would think very hard about who you want next to you right now, son."

I pinch the bridge of my nose, trying to quell the raging pain flowing through me.

"Dad. Leave." I don't hesitate. The sooner he's gone, the sooner I can lie down. Being in the hospital for a few days sucked. I could never get comfortable, and someone was always popping in to check on me. I get why, but it did not allow for a restful recovery.

With one last glare, he walks out the front door and slams it behind him.

"I forgot how charming your dad was." Peyton slips out from my grasp.

I head toward the couch and collapse on it. "Fuck. I missed being at home."

"What can I get you?" She sounds faraway now.

You, I want to say, *only you.*

But instead, I let sleep pull me under.

WHISPERED WORDS PULL ME AWAKE. Everything is hazy, but the throbbing in my head has dulled. Mostly.

Getting a concussion sucks.

"C'mon, Waffles. Let's go outside."

Puppy paws pattering through the halls put a smile on my face. Before, the house would've been empty. If it weren't for Peyton, my dad would be here. And that quiet would be even worse because it'd be filled with disapproving stares.

I'm glad I can't use any screens, because I'm sure there are several unread messages from my dad. No doubt telling me how I could've done a better job protecting myself from that hit.

Dragging myself off the couch, I head toward the backyard. Damn, if Peyton with my dog isn't a sight for sore eyes.

"Who's the best puppy?" Peyton is sitting cross-legged on the ground, while Waffles attacks her face with kisses. I watch as she throws the ball for him. He's not the best retriever yet, still getting caught up in sniffing everything around him.

"Hey."

Peyton's head snaps in my direction, brown hair glowing gold in the last of the late afternoon sun.

"Hey. How are you feeling?"

I cross the small yard, sitting next to her. "Better now that I've slept. In case I haven't said it, thank you."

"For what?"

I drop a kiss on her shoulder. "For being here. I don't know what I'd be doing right now if my dad were here."

"Seems not much has changed there."

I shake my head, picking at the blades of grass. "Still a dick because he couldn't hack it. Not all of us had great parents like you."

She smiles at me, taking my hand in hers. "They always missed you. You know my dad loved you. Didn't matter if you played football or not."

Peyton's family always loved me. Maybe if my dad had been less focused on football, we might actually have a relationship. On the best of days, it's strained. Nothing like what Peyton has with her family. I was always jealous of it.

Waffles bounces across the yard, flopping into my lap, pulling me from my spiraling thoughts. "Hey buddy. I've missed you." He showers my face in kisses. "He didn't bother you?"

"Your snoring was more of a bother than he was." Peyton laughs. "I forgot how loud you are."

I bury my face in Waffles's soft fur. "I think she's mixing the two of us up. I do not snore."

"Whatever you want to believe, Colin," she says with a smile.

"That's how you're going to play it?"

She lifts a shoulder, not a care in the world. "Nothing that isn't true."

Pushing her back on the grass, I find the ticklish spot on her side. Her shrieks send Waffles scurrying across the yard. "Take it back."

Peyton's lithe body moves beneath mine. I've barely moved, just hovering above her, yet it reminds me of less innocent things we could be doing, but can't.

"I can't take back what is true!" She giggles on the ground next to me.

God, I forgot how beautiful she was like this. I don't know if that's because my brain is still fuzzy or what.

Peyton is making the pain less sharp, almost like her

presence is healing every part of me that was empty without her these last few years. My fingers find her necklace, tracing the letters I know by heart.

"You're not leaving me?"

Her fingers thread through my hair. "Not until next weekend."

"What's next weekend?"

"I'm going camping. I still get a fall break, so I'm heading to the mountains."

"You're going by yourself?" I pop up, turning my eyes to meet hers. "That can't be safe."

Peyton sits up, pulling my head into her lap. "It's perfectly safe. I have a sat phone I take, I only stay on populated trails, and I stay in secure campgrounds."

I roll my eyes. "You're in the middle of the forest. How secure can it be?"

"Aww. Are you worried about me?" Peyton traces a finger down my face. It's calming.

"When you're doing something stupid? Yes."

That same finger traces around my lips, down my jaw, and circles back up to my forehead. "When do I ever do anything stupid?"

"Fine. You have a point. But I still don't like it."

"Then come with me."

"Really?" I perk up.

"You can bring Waffles. I'm sure he'd love to go camping."

"Crap. He's getting neutered next week. Nicole will have him for the weekend since I was going to be in Dallas for a game."

"How about we plan something later for all three of us then?"

Later. In the future. I like making plans with this woman.

"Sounds perfect."

"Then get your sleeping bag ready, because we're going camping."

Crap. I don't know if I thought this through.

Chapter Twenty-Three

PEYTON

"Are you sure you still want to come with me?"

Colin hefts the last of his bags in the back of my rented camper van. "I'm fine."

It's been two weeks since his concussion. I've barely left his side. I'm worried if I do, then something might happen. He keeps telling me I'm hovering, but I don't care.

"I just don't want too much stimulation for your brain."

"I don't think it's brain stimulation you should be worried about." Colin crowds behind me, his lips finding my neck.

"Are you even able to do that?"

Warm hands slide around my waist, dipping below the band of my leggings. "The doctor cleared me."

I lean back into his touch. "I feel like this is something I should have confirmed with him."

"You don't believe me?" His breath ghosts the shell of my ear, sending goose bumps rippling across my skin.

"I just want to be careful. That's all." My breath escapes me in a whoosh. Now that I'm letting myself feel these things for Colin, I can't help but want to keep him safe.

"Mmm." His lips find the beating pulse of my neck. "I promise you, I'm fine. Now, let's get going so we can spend a rare weekend off during football season."

A smile spreads across my face. "Music to my ears."

"Oh, down on football now, are you?" Colin swats my ass as I get in the van.

"Please." I roll my eyes at him as he settles in beside me. "I'm happy that you're coming with me to my favorite place."

"I never took you for a glamper." He eyes the back of the van behind me. With a small built-in kitchen and bed, it's much better than sleeping on the forest floor. "Although, I will say, I appreciate not having to sleep in a sleeping bag on the forest floor."

"I discovered them senior year. It's easier to pick up and go."

Colin angles the chair toward me. "And is that what you plan on doing? Picking up and going?"

The late morning traffic leaving the city isn't as bad as it could be, but it is still heavy. It's one of the few things I dislike about the city.

"After you left sophomore year, I spent the summer traveling out west and going to any national park I could think of."

I can feel his eyes on me, but I don't look at him. Not even a quick glance.

"You didn't stay around Knoxville?"

When I pull up to a stoplight, I chance a look at him. The confusion is clear as day on his face.

"I couldn't. Not when everything reminded me of you."

"Where did we go wrong?" Colin asks.

It's a question I've asked myself hundreds of times. Maybe if things hadn't become so intense so fast. Maybe if Colin had stayed when I needed him most. Maybe if I hadn't let him go.

But it wouldn't do us any good to dwell on the past. Not if we want a future together.

"Let's not talk about it this weekend, okay?"

"Sure, okay." His voice is muffled as I press on the gas. The mountains in the distance are rising up to meet us. Hopefully that will be the only distance this weekend.

"I FORGOT how much I love hiking."

"Oh yeah? And why's that?" I look over my shoulder at him, but I know exactly where his eyes are pointing behind those dark sunglasses. "C'mon, Colin!"

"What?" He shrugs as he walks closer to me. "I can't help but admire your ass. You've always had a great one."

Laughter rumbles out of me. After the weirdness in the van this morning, we found an ease that I always remembered having with Colin. It was what drew me to him.

"I guess some things never change."

"I don't think you'd like it if I did."

The next thing I know, I'm swept off my feet and am staring at Colin's ass.

"What the hell, Colin?!" I shriek as he runs up the path.

"Someone has to keep you on your toes."

Setting me down near the edge of the trail, we're hidden among the yellow Aspen trees. "And why do you think I need to be kept on my toes?"

I wrap my arms around him. The leaves whisper in the wind. The heat in Colin's eyes travels down my body.

"Because you need someone who doesn't agree with everything you say. Keeps life exciting for you." His finger trails down the V in my top. My skin, already flush from the hike, flares hot. "I like…"

His words trail off.

"Like what?"

"I like knowing that I still get this reaction from you. After all this time."

His finger finds the zipper at the top of my shirt and tugs it down, exposing my sports bra. My nipples pebble beneath the fabric.

"What are you doing? We can't do this here." There's no real strength in my words. Colin could throw me down on the trail and I'd be helpless to do anything but take everything he gives me.

"Are you sure about that?" Plump lips press a kiss to the corner of my mouth. "We haven't seen anyone for miles."

"We can't—"

Colin ends my argument with a searing kiss. My entire body is consumed by his.

The way his tongue strokes mine sends hot, pounding pulses straight to my aching core. My body, already hot from the sun, is ready to explode if he doesn't hurry and get his hands on my bare skin.

Hitching a leg over his hip, I pull him closer to me.

"Didn't want to do this, huh?" The laughter in his voice draws my eyes to him. I push his sunglasses up his nose, resting them on his head.

"Think you can be quick? I don't want to get caught. Wouldn't be a good look."

The cocky grin he gives me is all Colin. I feel it everywhere.

"Just you wait, Rocky. Just you wait."

Colin doesn't give me any more warning before he unwraps my leg from around him and then tugs my leggings down. The cool breeze against my overheated skin does nothing to help the simmering need I feel for him.

"Can you stay quiet, Peyton?" His lips travel down my neck, nibbling on my collarbone.

"Yes," I whisper.

Colin sinks a finger inside me, and I cover my mouth with my palm, stifling the moans escaping me. With my free hand, I find the bulge in his joggers, stroking it through the thick fabric.

"Fuck. I love your hands on me," he whispers, dragging his tongue along my neck. His thumb finds my clit, rubbing teasing circles around it.

"Not as much as I love yours." The bark of the tree digs into my back. With each thrust of Colin's finger, I'm getting closer to exploding.

But I want him to come with me.

Shoving my hand into his pants, I find his hard length, ready and leaking for me.

"It won't take much. I've been wanting to be with you for the last two weeks."

Colin shifts, his eyes raking over my heated skin. He pushes the fabric of my bra down and takes my breast in hand.

I'm ready to tip right over the cliff. I thumb the slit of his cock, wanting to take him with me.

"Kiss me," I whisper. We're breathing each other in as we both explode. Hot cum coats my hand as Colin kisses me through my own orgasm. He tugs my lip between his teeth, prolonging the pleasure coursing through me.

"God, that felt good." Colin steps away, tucking

himself back into his joggers. He rights my clothes, kissing each spot as they hide away from his view.

"You're telling me." My eyes are shut as I'm resting against the tree, my entirely body boneless as Colin digs a wet wipe out of his pack and gently cleans my hand.

Colin drops a kiss on my neck, bringing me back to life. "Want to head back?"

I nod, wrapping him into my side as we find the trail. He's laughing to himself.

"What?"

"And you wondered why I love hiking."

Chapter Twenty-Four

COLIN

"I miss Waffles."

"Waffles your dog, or waffles the food?" Peyton gives me a cheeky smile.

"I'm serious. He would love this. Poor little guy getting his balls chopped off." I wince just thinking about it.

"He'll be fine. He's in good hands with Nicole this weekend until you can bring him home."

"I've gotten used to having the little guy around."

Peyton relaxes into my hold. The campground is surprisingly empty. The weather has been beautiful up until an hour ago when dark clouds started moving in.

"I promise you, we'll come back another weekend with him."

"I like the sound of that." My lips find her hair. The thought of having any future with Peyton is something I never imagined.

After how things ended between us, I never thought this was a possibility. I spent those first weeks in Denver in a haze. I went balls to the wall with off-season workouts, because anything was better than missing Peyton. I know I should let the past lie, but I can't. I know it will just lurk around the edges.

"What happened between us, Peyton?"

Her body stiffens in my arms. "Is this really the time to talk about it?"

"Don't you think we need to in order to move forward?"

"Look at you, acting like a grown-up."

I stifle a laugh. "It was bound to happen at some point."

Peyton sighs but doesn't say anything else. A cold breeze blows through the campground. The mountains are no longer visible in the distance, hiding behind the clouds.

"Why'd you leave me?" I ask quietly.

She shifts in my arms. "You left me." Her brown eyes are piercing. "Why do you keep saying I left? One day you were at school, and the next thing I knew you were being drafted by Denver. It crushed me."

"Because you pushed me away!"

"How did I push you away?" Peyton stands, hands on her hips. Anger pulses off her. The wind whips her hair around her face.

"Don't you remember the letter you wrote me?"

If I thought she was angry before, it has nothing on her now. My little spitfire. "Don't you mean the letter you wrote me? You told me things got too intense after the pregnancy scare and that you needed to concentrate on football and were going into the draft."

What in the actual fuck? "Are you kidding me? You told me things were too intense and that I should go out for the draft because you needed to focus on school. You thought I'd bail after I held your hand when that condom broke and you thought you were pregnant? That'd be next level asshole."

"We were kids, Colin!" Peyton shouts. "Neither one of us was ready to deal with a baby. Thank God the test was negative, because you couldn't be bothered to stick around."

"I couldn't be bothered? You sent me packing," I huff. The first drop of rain hits me on the forehead, but I ignore it. "I can recite that letter forward and backward, Peyton. It gutted me that you didn't need me anymore. You said things got too intense after that and you didn't want to be together."

"I did no such thing! Why wouldn't I want you by my side through all of that? I was a wreck that entire summer. I couldn't stand being anywhere that reminded me of you, so I packed up and left. I was tempted to transfer, but my parents wouldn't let me. So why in the world would I send you away?"

"You really didn't write me that letter?" I take a breath, calmer now. Peyton's shoulders have almost sagged in defeat.

"No, Colin. The last thing I ever wanted was for you to leave."

I take a step toward her as the rain starts to get heavier. Brown locks cling to her face. "So then who wanted to break us up?"

"You really can't think of anyone?" I hate how bitter she sounds.

"There's no way he would do that."

"And yet, you know immediately who I'm talking about."

I wipe the rain out of my eyes. "Just because my dad wasn't supportive of our relationship doesn't mean he broke us up."

"He looked at me like I was shit on the bottom of his

shoe when he saw me last week. This is why I didn't want to get into it."

Peyton goes to turn her back, but I grab her arm, stopping her. "Don't walk away. Not again."

There's a fire in her eyes that I've missed. Fuck, it was one of the things I loved most about her. "I never walked away the first time."

That's it. That's all it takes for me to crash my lips to hers. I swallow her gasp as I meld her body to mine. The warmth of her mouth heats me from the inside out, acting as a shield from the cold rain.

We could spark the air around us, we're so on edge. Every stroke of my tongue against hers has my dick thickening behind my zipper.

All I want is her. Peyton. She's all I've ever wanted. Even when I couldn't have her.

Our kiss becomes less frantic, but no less intense as I back Peyton up against the van. A boom of thunder in the distance has me pulling back.

"Maybe we should get inside?"

Peyton's eyes are hazy, her lips swollen from my kisses. With the rain dripping from her eyelashes, she's the sexiest fucking woman I've ever seen.

I open the door and pull her in behind me, thankful for the room this thing has. A shiver racks her body.

"Let me warm you up."

I pull her toward me. The Henley shirt she wears clings to her every curve. I peel the damp material off of her. Her skin pebbles against the cool air. Brushing a stray lock of hair behind her ear, I dip my head, kissing the water droplets off her face.

Her body sways into me. "Colin."

The glare of her necklace catches on the lights. *Rocky.* "I love that you still wear this."

It's a nickname I gave her because she loved the mountains. It slipped out on our first date, and it was the only thing I called her. The necklace couldn't have been more than twenty bucks when I got it for her, but she loved it.

And I love seeing it on her still.

"I never stopped loving you."

"God, me either."

Peyton's lips find mine, searching and taking whatever she wants from this kiss. I give it to her. I try to show her how I feel through this kiss. With each touch of my hands on her body.

My mouth blazes a warm path down her body, licking and sucking on her exposed skin. Peyton's hands sink into my hair, guiding me farther south.

The scent of her vanilla body wash lingers. I forgot how good she tastes. I drop to my knees, untying her boots and tossing them behind me.

"You look so fucking sexy like this. Ready for me to take you." I nip at her hipbone. Running a finger under the waistband of her leggings, I snap it back. The small gasp from Peyton tells me she likes it. I slide the tight pants down her legs, letting them pool at her feet. I kiss a trail back up one leg, nipping at the soft skin of her inner thigh.

"Get on the bed." I drop a kiss just above her underwear.

Kicking out of her pants, Peyton turns and watches me as she crosses the short distance to the bed. "What are you waiting for?"

The breathiness in her voice has me stripping down to my boxers and crossing to her. Every inch we're apart is one inch too many. I don't ever want to be away from this woman again.

Pulling her to the edge of the bed, I take in the sexy creature in front of me.

The swell of her tits.

The way her lips are swollen.

How her hand is now sliding behind the swath of fabric covering her pussy.

"Hey now." I grab her hand and pull it up to my mouth, sucking her fingers inside. "That's my job."

"Then hurry. I need you."

I need you. Now my favorite words in the English language.

I swirl my tongue around the pads of her fingers, tasting just how much she does want me. I groan around her. My cock is painfully hard. I could find a quick release with her, but I want to draw out her pleasure. I want every ounce of her desire.

I trail kisses down her leg, sucking at the soft skin just below where she really wants me. I feather my breath over her pussy as she's writhing beneath me.

"Colin!"

"Patience, Rocky, patience." I lick a path at the apex of her thigh. Teasing Peyton was always one of my favorite things. And based on how she's reacting right now, she hates it. But I have no intentions of stopping.

"You're killing me here!"

Glancing up, I see her grabbing her hair in lustful frustration.

"Where do you want me?" I lower my head to her pussy and lick a path up the fabric. "Here?"

I move up her body, sucking a nipple into my mouth through the fabric of her bra. "Or here?"

"Yes!" Peyton shrieks.

"Yes to what?" I pull back and rub the growing bulge behind my boxers.

"Everything. I want it all. I want you everywhere."

I cover her body with mine as I expose her left breast, the nipple diamond hard. "Everywhere it is."

I take my time. Flicking and sucking the tight bud, I give Peyton everything I have. I play with the other one, rolling it between my thumb and forefinger.

"You always used to like this. Think you could come just from me playing with your tits?"

"You know I can." She tilts her head up. The challenge is there.

Oh, it's on.

Pushing up onto my elbows, I trail a wet path across her cleavage to her other tit. Sucking it between my teeth, I tug on it. "Don't stop. Don't stop, don't stop, don't stop."

My smile is evil. I know Peyton's close based on how her body is moving beneath mine.

I continue my efforts, letting one hand drift down her stomach to hold her there. The rain is loud on top of the van, but it does nothing to stifle the moans and gasps that Peyton is making.

It's making my dick ache. There's nothing I want more than to be inside her, but I want her to come first. My cock can wait. Peyton is more important right now.

I circle my tongue around her nipple, lazy strokes that finally push her over the edge.

"God, yes!" Her fingers find my hair, holding my head to her as she chases her pleasure. My eyes move up to see her blissed-out face.

"I sound like a broken record, but fuck, you're stunning when you come like that."

"I like it when you make me come like that."

I slide up her body, my mouth a magnet to hers as I give her a punishing kiss. Her body is lax under mine as I flip us around. "Think you can do it again?"

Peyton is glowing. Her hair falls in waves around us. It

feels like we're the only two people in the world. Soft fingers trace a pathway down the ridges in my abs. My dick is perking up the closer she gets to him.

"I think I can manage." Peyton wraps her hand my dick and my back flies off the bed. It feels like forever since she's had her hands on me when it's only been a few hours. I'm greedy for her touch. Now that I have it, I never want to lose it.

"Fuck me, that's amazing."

"Isn't that what you want me to do?" Her eyes are glittering.

"You better hurry, because I don't think I'll last."

Peyton shifts so she's straddling me. Her fist is tight around me, but her strokes are lazy. "I like seeing you all worked up like this."

I have to take deep breaths so I don't come in her hand. I want to be buried inside her. Feel her tight heat around me as she rides me.

"Get moving, Rocky. I want to feel you come on my cock." My hands find her hips, urging her forward. She takes the hint, grabbing a condom from the table and sheathing my dick. Then she lines herself up and sinks down onto me, and it takes everything I have not to jack-knife off the bed.

"You look incredible." Her skin is flushed from her earlier orgasm as she swivels her hips over me.

"You *feel* incredible." Peyton starts moving. With each shift of her hips, I'm that much closer to exploding inside her. God, she really feels amazing.

"Fuck. I'm so close, Rocky."

I should be embarrassed by how close I am to coming, but I'm not. Not with Peyton. Her movements become frenzied, and I know she is just as close as I am.

She reaches down to swipe her fingers over her clit,

and I know I'm a goner. As soon as she starts to contract around me, I'm exploding.

"Fuck!" I growl. Thunder vibrates the van as we both come together. Peyton holds herself over me as her orgasm moves through her. Her head is thrown back in pleasure as her release washes over her.

Peyton sags against me, our skin slick with sweat. "Why is every time better than the last?" Her breath washes over my pec as I drag a lazy finger up and down her back.

"It's always been like that."

Resting a hand on my chest, she turns her head to look up at me. "It was, wasn't it?"

We're both quiet. The storm outside lessens as we lie together in bed, almost like it was what was building between the two of us. Whoever was trying to keep us apart before isn't going to be an issue. I won't let some stupid letters come between us.

"Promise we won't let anything come between us again?" Peyton's words that seem to echo my own thoughts are so quiet, I almost miss them.

"Never."

God, not if I can help it.

Because now that I have Peyton again, I never plan on letting her go.

Chapter Twenty-Five

PEYTON

"Peyton. Are you coming to the Thanksgiving luncheon?" Tammy pops her head around my cubicle.

"I was planning on it."

"Good. Are you going home for Thanksgiving?"

I shake my head. "No. My parents are going to visit my brother and his family, so I'm staying here this year. It'll be nice to have a few days off."

Tammy smiles at me. "You've been doing a great job. Earl has been very impressed with your work."

"Thanks, Tammy. I really enjoy working here."

"Keep it up, and I'll see you later at the luncheon."

It's hard to keep the smile off my face. It's been a few weeks since Colin's concussion. We haven't spent much time apart since. And today he'll hear from the team about whether he can play this week.

Concussion protocol is no joke.

Before I get too lost in my thoughts, Earl appears above the short wall of my workspace. "Got a minute?"

I smile at him. "Sure."

Following behind him, I try not to let my nerves get the best of me.

"Have a seat, Peyton." Earl shuts the door behind me.

"Is everything okay?" I put more strength into my voice than I actually feel. Nothing like an impromptu meeting with your boss to make you feel like you're going to get fired.

Earl gives me a warm smile, settling some of my nerves. "Tammy has been singing your praises."

I sigh. "She has?"

"Absolutely. And Suzanne, the team Communications Director, has been thrilled with Colin's progress."

"He's been doing a great job."

It was a bumpy start to say the least. Thank God things changed, but who knows where the two of us would be otherwise.

Earl chuckles. "It can be hard if people don't want to change. Luckily Colin's lack of time in the tabloids has been a good thing."

"Hopefully that lifestyle is a thing of the past."

"I wanted to commend you on your work. If you keep this up, we'll have a spot for you after graduation."

"That would be great."

Except dread settles in my stomach. I'm breaking the one rule Earl told me was nonnegotiable. Sleeping with the client.

"I'll let you get going, but just wanted to let you know you're doing a great job."

I stand, a fake smile plastered on my face. "Thank you, Earl. I appreciate it."

I take his proffered hand and quickly make my exit.

Not paying attention, I run smack into a hard body. One I'm intimately familiar with.

"Hey, Rocky." That pearly-white grin only ratchets up the nerves I'm feeling. "What's wrong?"

His voice drops the moment he notices my face. Colin grabs my arm and pulls me into an empty conference room.

"Earl told me I was doing a good job with you." I long to reach out and touch him. To let him calm me in a way that only he can.

"And that's a bad thing?" Colin lifts my chin to meet his gaze.

I take a step back from him. It's hard to breathe when he's in my space. That woodsy, lavender scent always overwhelms me in the best way.

"We aren't supposed to be together, Colin. This could be bad for both of us."

"What are you saying, Peyton?" I don't miss the note of fear as he speaks.

I never thought I'd get a second chance with Colin. It was never a possibility. But now that I have him, it's getting harder and harder to keep what we have between the two of us. Colin lives in the public eye. It's only a matter of time before someone figures it out.

"I'm worried this won't last between us. And what happens if I lose my job?"

Colin glances around before pulling me deeper into the conference room. No one can see us in here with the frosted glass walls.

"We're being careful, Peyton. It's not like we're going out to clubs every night."

"But what if someone sees us?"

"Who is going to see us?"

I lean into Colin, needing support from him. "I just don't want anything to come between us, and it feels like the world is trying to keep us apart."

Warm hands thread through my hair. Colin whispers into my ear, "Do you think that I'm going to let anyone keep us apart now that I have you?"

"But—"

"No buts, Peyton."

I drop my forehead to his chest. His heartbeat is steady, unlike mine that is beating out of control. "This is quite the change in roles."

"What do you mean?"

Colin's fingers play with the hair at the nape of my neck. It's soothing. It takes everything I have not to groan in delight.

"I was always the one trying to keep you calm. Now it's you. Never thought that would happen."

"Isn't that what people call growth?" His laugh soothes me instantly.

I pull back from him, staring into those blue eyes I love so much. "Only took you twenty-six years. I'm so proud."

"Gotta shape up sometime, Rocky."

I look around, making sure we're still alone. Standing on my tiptoes, I press a quick kiss to Colin's lips. Deep down, I know in my gut I shouldn't even do this, but right now, I need some reassurance.

"Are you going to be okay?" Colin kisses my forehead.

I puff out a breath, trying to force some reassurance into my words. "I guess I just needed to hear it from you."

"I'll tell you as often as you need me to."

This time, I steal a longer kiss, letting his lips do the soothing.

"We should go before people come looking for you," Colin whispers. Except he makes no move to leave.

"You're probably right."

"Are you still coming over tonight?"

I nod. "Yes. I'll be over after the luncheon. You're still meeting with the team doctor, right?"

He gives me a reassuring smile. "Should be cleared to play on Sunday."

And just like that, the nerves come back.

"How many times have you seen me play, Peyton?" Colin asks. He takes a step back, leaning against the conference room table. The distance helps this time.

"More than I can count."

He nods. "And you know concussion protocol. I'll be fine."

"Doesn't mean I still won't worry."

Colin extends a hand to me, and I willingly go. His palms are rough from years of football. His gaze darts to the door and back to me.

"I'll always do my best to be as safe as I can on the field. I know it's not something I can promise, but I'll do my best. So try not to worry, okay?"

"Okay."

"Good." Colin smirks at me. "Then let's go out there and pretend like we're not going to see each other naked all weekend."

Chapter Twenty-Six

COLIN

"So who do we need to win today?" Peyton settles onto the couch next to me, Waffles on my other side. Instead of a big Thanksgiving dinner, we loaded up on junk food. Just like we used to do in college.

"Detroit. It'll put us in the best position when we play San Francisco this week."

"Are you excited to be back on the field?" Peyton pops a chip into her mouth.

I nod. "So fucking ready. I hate not being out there with the guys."

I'd never been so happy to see the team doctor as I was yesterday. Sitting out for a few weeks was rough.

"You'll be there, right?"

Peyton smiles, leaning into my side as the game kicks off. "You couldn't keep me away."

I can't hide my reaction. Burying my face into her neck, I pepper her with kisses. "I fucking love you. You know that, right?"

She shrugs her shoulder. "I guess. But I'll never get tired of hearing you say it."

Pulling back, I cup her cheeks. "I love you."

It's the first time I've said those exact words since we started this thing between us. But I've loved her every minute we were apart, and even more now that we're back together.

The whistle on the TV blows, starting the game.

"I love you, Colin. We found each other again in the weirdest way, but I'm glad we did."

The game plays in the background, as we alternate kissing and snacking. At some point, Waffles wanders off to his bed in the office, tired of watching the game. I love my dog, but a football fan he is not.

"Running back is going to get the ball," Peyton chirps, popping a chip into her mouth.

I nearly spit out my beer. "No way. Quarterback is definitely going to keep it."

Peyton shakes her head. "With the read option? Detroit's quarterback always goes with the handoff."

Grabbing the remote, I pause the TV. "Want to bet on it?"

Peyton shifts on the couch, crossing her legs under her. "What do you have in mind?"

I know a devious smile is spreading across my face as I gaze at her. Neither of us put much effort into what we're wearing. Sweats and T-shirts. Nothing fancy since it's just the two of us.

"For every play I get right, you take off a piece of clothing. For every play you get right, I take off a piece of clothing."

Peyton shakes her head. "No way. You'll be naked in thirty seconds."

"Ouch. You think I'm that bad at the game I play?"

A cocky smile spreads across Peyton's face. God, this is

one more of the things I love about her. Her competitive side.

"No, I'm just that good."

"Fine then. How about every scoring play after this one?"

"You're on." Peyton extends a hand to me.

"Prepare to take off your shirt."

Resuming the game, we watch the play unfold. Defense picks up the linebacker, making an easy route for the quarterback to hand off the ball to his running back.

Fuck.

"Yes! Told you he'd go to the running back. In your face, James!" Peyton rises up on her knees in celebration. "Give me your pants."

Peyton wiggles her ass in my face. Giving it a hardy smack, I stand.

"I can't believe I didn't get that right."

I strip out of my sweats, throwing them in Peyton's face. Her laugh warms me from the inside out.

"You pay more attention to the defense, not the offense. And Detroit's quarterback hasn't had good luck keeping the ball."

Fuck, if Peyton rattling off football stats like this isn't making me hard.

I adjust myself, sitting down on the couch. Detroit is in the red zone, within twenty yards of the end zone.

"Alright, what do you call here?" I pause the TV again.

Peyton stands, going over to the TV and studying the line. "Hey! You can't look that closely," I complain.

"What? I have to get a read on what they're doing."

"I'm starting it. Call it."

I don't want to give Peyton any advantage. Girl knows her football.

"Fine. Out route to the receiver for a touchdown."

"Handoff to the running back," I counter, hitting the play button.

The game starts and the QB hands it off to the running back. The offensive line holds the defense and he bursts through, running easily into the end zone.

"Fuck yeah!" I pump my arms. "Lose the shirt."

Peyton grumbles, pulling her shirt off over her head. Her nipples are hard under her bra, joggers sitting low on her curvy hips.

"How does it feel to lose?"

Crossing her arms, Peyton glares at me. "I haven't lost yet."

"We'll see."

The game continues, on screen and off. Peyton wins, then I win, slowly dropping our clothes. We've moved from our spots on the couch, standing in front of the TV like two crazy people. We're both down to our underwear. We're chest to chest. Every brush of her nipples against me has my dick hardening in my briefs.

"Last play before the half. Call it." My eyes gaze down at hers. The tension is high. I can see in her eyes how much she doesn't want to lose.

"Long bomb to the end zone for Detroit to tie the game."

I eye the TV, looking at the play. "Philly is going to stop them."

Peyton shakes her head. "That's too easy."

"It's what's going to happen."

Quirking a brow, Peyton turns toward the TV, arms crossed in front of her. Her tits rest perfectly on top of her arms. I move behind her, letting her feel how hard I am.

I rest my hands on Peyton's hips, pulling her back into me as the play unfolds before us. The quarterback escapes the pocket but runs right into a linebacker.

"You know what that means."

"I can't believe I lost," Peyton grumbles.

"Mmm, yes. Just terrible." I drop kisses along her neck and shoulder. "We need to lose these."

Dipping my hands inside her underwear, I push them down. Peyton stands still, not moving.

"You're not being very cooperative." I trail kisses down her spine, feeling each ridge as I go.

"Maybe you need to work a little harder then." Peyton wiggles her hips.

"Is that it?"

I nibble on the soft flesh of her ass. Her moans tell me she likes it.

"You like that?" I do the same to the other side.

"No."

"Is this how you're going to play it?" I stand, pressing into her.

She doesn't answer. I drag my fingers up her sides, brushing the underside of her gorgeous tits.

"Maybe if I actually enjoyed it."

"Something tells me you do." Her nipples pebble as I move my calloused palms over them. She's biting down on her bottom lip, trying to fight it.

I pull her diamond-hard tip between my fingers, rolling it as a loud moan escapes her.

"Is this you not liking it?" I go to pull my hand away, but hers flies up, keeping it there.

"Hate it," she sighs.

Moving both my hands down, I spin her in my arms and take her mouth in a bruising kiss. I love how her lips feel against mine. But Peyton isn't backing down. She's fighting to control this kiss.

I know it's driving her crazy that she lost. I can feel it as she swipes her tongue over mine. I'll let her have this moment. Because I'm going to drive her wild before I'm done with her.

"You know, you're not a very good loser," I whisper, once I'm able to peel my lips away from hers.

"And you're a cocky winner."

Peyton's hands skate down my chest, toying with the waistband of my briefs. If my cock wasn't hard before, it's a steel pipe now.

But that's not where my mind is right now. Sinking down to my knees, I breathe in the sweet scent of her pussy.

"When I have this as a prize?" Pulling her leg onto my shoulder, I open her wide to me. I swipe my tongue through her wetness, loving the taste of her on my tongue. "Yeah, I'm cocky."

"Fuck, that feels good." Peyton drops her head back.

Her hands land in my hair, keeping me locked in place. My tongue keeps stroking, as I add two fingers, moving inside her tight heat.

"Oh God, I'm so close!" Peyton's leg pulls me in tighter.

I don't let up. I want Peyton to have at least one orgasm before she's coming on my cock. I never used to consider myself possessive of an orgasm, but with Peyton? I want them all. I want to be the only person to ever bring her this kind of pleasure. To see her like this.

Sucking her clit into my mouth, her shouts tell me she's coming. I wrap a hand around her waist, holding her to me as she rides my face. I know I am leaking precum everywhere because this woman has me so hard.

When the rush passes, I stand, sucking my fingers into my mouth. Peyton's eyes, crazy with lust, watch me.

"Still don't like losing?" I whisper, dropping an innocent kiss on her lips. I let my lips hover over hers, her soft whimpers hot on my own mouth.

"I'm not sure how this is me losing." Peyton leans her head back to look me in the eye but stays pressed to my chest.

My gaze rakes over her. Nipples hard. Chest flushed. Mouth swollen from my kiss.

"You're right. But I still think I need to claim my prize."

"And what's that?" Peyton runs a hand down my chest, pushing my briefs down to my ankles.

"Me inside of you."

Peyton's hand brushes over my hardened length, just enough to tease.

"Is that so?"

A clever gleam sparks in her eyes before she sinks to her knees and swallows my aching dick.

"Fuck. This isn't what I had in mind."

Yet, I can't bring myself to care. With Peyton's lips wrapped around my dick, it's pure bliss. If this was the only kind of sex we had for the rest of our lives, I couldn't bring myself to care.

Well, maybe a little bit.

The faster she moves, the closer and closer I get to coming. And I don't want to be coming down her throat.

"Stop." With more force than necessary, I pull her off of me. Peyton looks more than pleased with herself, but before she knows what's happening, I'm dragging her over to the couch and sitting down.

"Is this you claiming your prize?"

"Fuck yes. I want you riding me."

Peyton straddles my hips, taking my slick cock in her hand. "Condom?"

I shake my head. "Last test was negative. I'm good if you're good."

Peyton smiles and nods her head. "Me too."

When she slides down me, I about damn near explode.

Being inside her tight heat feels fucking phenomenal. I run a single finger down her chest, sweeping under her tit and up around her nipple. She whimpers.

"Why does this feel so right?"

Shoving a hand into her hair, I bring her gaze to mine. "Because it's you and me, Rocky. Nothing has ever been more right than that."

I bring her lips to mine, anchoring her to me as she starts to rock. Each swivel of her hips, taking me deeper, has us both reaching the brink faster than we want.

"I need you to come again."

"I'm right there." Our breaths mix as I feel Peyton clench around me. It tips me over the edge as I spill into her.

"Fuck." I draw the word out, holding Peyton close as pleasure courses through both of us.

"How does it get better every time?" I whisper into Peyton's neck. Sweat sticks to her slick skin.

"I don't know. But God, it really does get better every time."

I kiss my way up her neck. "I'll take that as a compliment."

"Why did I know you'd be cocky about that?"

I flip us around so Peyton is on the couch beneath me. "What can I say? I love knowing how good I make it for you."

Peyton's fingers brush down my face, tracing my lips. "I know I shouldn't say it because it'll go to your head, but it's only ever been this good with you."

I fight the instinct to say "of course," which would give

her what she expects. But I feel the same way. It's one of the many reasons I was with all those women.

"You're the only person who has ever made me feel like this too."

"Always have to win, don't you?" she asks.

"If this was you losing, I'll take it any day of the week."

Chapter Twenty-Seven

COLIN

"**A**re you ready to get back out there?" Coach asks me, walking up to my locker. I've missed being in here, surrounded by the guys. There's nothing like the energy here on game day.

"More than ready."

It's been six weeks. Six long weeks of sitting at home and watching my team play. The Mountain Lions didn't want me on the sidelines. So I'm itching to get back out there.

"You'll be starting, but you might not get to play every snap."

"Coach—"

He cuts me off. "No arguments. I know you've been practicing and have been cleared, but I still don't want you taking any unnecessary hits."

I grumble, flipping my gloves from hand to hand.

"Understood?" He levels me with a look that says, *if you want to play, this is the only way.*

"Understood."

As soon as Coach Brooks walks away, the guys are all

crowding around me. "I can't wait to have you back out there on the field," Alex says, pulling me into a hug. "We've missed you."

"I even started getting more reps. And I only liked it a little bit," Logan admits with a laugh.

"I can't wait until we play Vegas again." There's a gleam in Knox's eye that tells me he wishes he could lay their guy out cold.

"I'm so fucking happy to be back on the field." I clap each of them on the shoulder.

"And your head is feeling good?" Alex takes it between his hands, looking at me like I might have a concussion.

"Relax." I swat his arms away. "I've been well taken care of for the last few weeks."

It sucked not being able to play and being away from the guys, but it brought Peyton and me closer together. I know she's still hesitant on how things are going to work for us, but she's who I want. Football and Peyton.

"Then how about we get out there and show the fans what they've been missing?" Alex says.

"Fuck yeah!" I follow them out of the locker room and wait in the tunnel.

"You're out last, Colin. The fans want to welcome you back," Coach says as he walks out onto the field.

"Hell yeah!"

I'm revving to go. One by one, the starting offense is called out onto the field. The anticipation builds.

After Alex is announced, I'm there, waiting to be called when I hear the announcer welcome me into the raucous stadium.

"Denver fans, get on your feet! Let's welcome back our wide receiver. Number eighty-seven, from Tennessee... COLIN JAMES!"

Running through the fog machines onto the field is the

best feeling in the world. Fans are chanting my name as I wave to everyone. Cheerleaders line the field as I run toward the huddle.

This feeling, hearing my name announced to the crowd?

I fucking love it.

"Let's do this, boys!" I yell to the team.

We head to the sidelines as the pregame rituals start. My eyes drift toward the spot in the stands where I know Peyton is sitting. I got a picture of her in my jersey before I got to the stadium.

My number never looked so good.

Alex comes back after winning the coin toss and receiving the ball. I'm ready to get back out there and show these fans I'm good as new.

And that's exactly what we do.

Winning by a score of 38-20.

Chapter Twenty-Eight

COLIN

"**D**oes everyone understand the rules?" Peyton asks, looking around the group.

"So let me get this straight." A redhead in Alex's group holds her hand up. "We run around like crazy people, trying to find places in Denver based on clues, find the person there to help us, and the first team to get to the brewery wins?"

It's only because I know Peyton so well that I see the *duh* look on her face. "Yes! Every team has to work together. And only walking or bikes to get around."

It's surprisingly warm for early December in Denver. When Peyton arranged this scavenger hunt to raise funds for the team's local charity, I was skeptical at first. I didn't know how this would help me, until she told me she arranged for the local news to cover the event.

It had Earl eating out of the palm of her hand.

And he's not the only one.

"Colin. Before we get started, do you mind if I ask you a few questions?" The local reporter, Kelsie, will be following along with our group. I convinced Peyton to come along with our team instead of waiting at the end.

"Sure thing." I give her my media-ready smile.

"A lot has been said these last few weeks about how you're seen around town."

I keep my smile plastered on my face. "And where have you seen me around town?"

She smiles. Her teeth are so white, there is no way they are natural. "Aside from these charity events, no one *has* seen you around. What has brought about that change?"

Looking down, I hide the smile that I know is a goofy grin. Peyton brings it out in me. I clear my throat before looking up at her. "I realized what was important in life and made the decision to change. I'm not the same kid I was when Denver first drafted me, so I want to show the team that matters to me, what matters most in my life. Helping others. Playing football. Being a good teammate."

"The fans are loving it. They all want to know if you're still single." Kelsie gives me a hopeful smile.

"The fans, Kelsie, or you?" I pop an eyebrow at her.

Peyton interrupts the conversation. "Thanks, Kelsie. We need to go ahead and get started."

"Oh, sure." She looks disappointed, but I'm thankful for the interruption.

"How'd you know I needed the save?" I whisper, looking straight ahead at the group we're working with.

"I guessed."

"You guessed? Or you were jealous I was talking to someone that wasn't you?" I bump my shoulder against hers.

"Contrary to popular belief, not every woman is jealous of every other woman a man looks at. I just didn't want her asking probing questions that wouldn't reflect well on you in the article she's writing."

"Damn, Rocky. You're good."

Peyton spins on her heel, walking backward toward our group. "What can I say? It's why I get all the good jobs with Earl."

It strikes a chord. Earl brought us together, and yet, he's the very reason we can't be together. I would love nothing more than to wrap her in my arms and hold her hand as we do this ridiculous scavenger hunt, but I can't.

And if she gets a full-time job with Earl? I'd have no idea how to navigate those treacherous seas. She's an unpaid intern, getting credit for her master's degree. As a full-time employee? There's no way we could be together.

An uneasy feeling washes over me. "You ready to get started?"

Peyton eyes me. I know she senses the change. Tension builds at the base of my neck. The last thing I need is a headache coming over this. It's not like we can change anything right this second.

She nods, calling out to the rest of the teams. "Alright. Is everyone ready?"

Cheers and whoops are heard around us, as each team is ready to get started.

"Let's go!" Peyton shouts, and teams tear open the envelopes they've been given.

WHAT PART *of Denver is marked as Mile High? Find this spot for your next clue!*

"That's easy! State Capitol Building!" Logan whispers to me.

Gotta love the kid. When I was telling the other captains about the event, he didn't want to be left out and joined my team.

Teams are rushing off around us.

"According to GPS, it's a ten-minute walk from here," Audrey says.

Logan invited her to join him. I knew something was up between the two of them at the home opener, but this confirms it.

"Quicker if we run!" Logan shouts.

Our group takes off sprinting, Peyton and I jogging lightly behind them.

"You didn't tell me this was going to be a day of strenuous activity." I wink at Peyton.

"I can't help it if a bunch of athletes are competitive when they get together."

"If I had known this is what we'd be doing, I'd have suggested some other more fun activities to work up the heart rate."

We slow down as we approach a red light.

"Keep your voice down!" Peyton's head swivels around, making sure no one heard me.

"Relax. We're fine." Other groups are running across the street.

Her cheeks are flushed from the short run. "What if someone hears you and word gets back to Earl? What then?"

"I don't know, Peyton." I tell her the truth. "But if you go to work for him, we'll have to figure something out."

"I don't see how we can." Her voice is dejected as she crosses the street, leaving me behind.

The slouch in her shoulders matches how I'm feeling about us right now. Because really, where can we go?

Shaking off the stupor, I follow the rest of my team. Three groups are ahead of us. I have no idea if the rest of the clues are random or not as two teams take off in different directions. Logan and Audrey find the person on the Capitol steps and grab our next envelope.

"I'm feeling blue. Can you give me a big bear hug?" Audrey says out loud. "Feeling blue?"

Peyton stands with us, not answering since she created the clues.

"What the hell is blue?" Logan asks out loud.

Kelsie grabs my arm. "The Blue Bear at the Convention Center!"

"Genius!" the last member of our team shouts, and everyone takes off again.

It's less than a mile, but my enthusiasm has now been zapped.

I'm winning over the fans of Denver. The team is loving me. But can I continue to have the one person love me who can't be allowed to?

Things were so much easier in college when it was just the two of us.

Chapter Twenty-Nine

PEYTON

"Peyton, Earl wants to see you in his office." The hardness of Tammy's voice sets me on edge. She's been nothing but friendly to me the entire time I've been working here. This tone has a chill spreading down my spine.

"Sure thing." I grab my notebook, steeling my nerves as I make my way into Earl's office. He doesn't look happy.

Shit. This can't be good.

"What did you want to see me about, Earl?" I inject as much courage as I can muster into my voice.

"It's not good news, Peyton." He's shaking his head. "I'm afraid I'm going to have to let you go."

A lead weight settles in my belly.

"Has my performance been unsatisfactory?" There's a wobble to my voice. I couldn't hold it back if I wanted to.

"No. And that's what makes this so difficult." Earl clasps his hands together, leaning over his desk. "It's come to my attention that you have been seeing one of the clients."

"Okay." I try to swallow, but can't. How in the world

did he find out? Colin and I were careful. We were always careful.

But can one ever fully hide their true feelings for someone they love?

"Peyton. I have rules for a reason. It's easy to get swept up with people making big promises to you. I've seen too many people crash and burn because they took these sports stars at their word. It causes huge headaches, and it's not worth it."

I nod, my eyes flooding with tears. The last thing I want to do is cry in front of Earl.

"Can I ask how you found out about this?"

Earl's brow pinches together. "The fact that you're not denying it tells me all I need to know."

"I don't think it'd do me any favors at this point to deny it." This time, a single tear gets free. I wipe it away, frustrated at the position I now find myself in.

"I have these rules for a reason, Peyton. I wish it hadn't come to this, but I can't treat you any differently."

I nod. "I understand. I appreciate the opportunity you've given me." I stand, ready to put this office behind me.

"You've got a very bright future ahead of you, and I wish you well." Earl gives me a tight smile as I leave.

It feels like every pair of eyes is on me as I make my way back to my cubicle to grab my bag.

Everything that I was worried about finally happened.

Did I will it into happening?

Colin was nothing but sure that everything would be okay.

But right now, it's so far from okay.

At the start of the semester, my future was right there, ready for me to grab.

Now, it's a blur. I have no internship. No college credit.

How in the world am I going to make my dream come true now?

Colin

"IT'S GOING to be okay, Waffles."

I've been pacing my living room since Peyton texted that she was on her way over. It's the middle of the day, so I can't imagine it's for a good reason. She told me she had to be in the office this week, so it's ratcheting my nerves up even higher.

My gut reaction was to check the news for something that got out. On us or maybe me—I wasn't sure what I was looking for.

But there was nothing.

Whatever reason Peyton has for coming here now likely isn't good.

A soft knock at the door has me rushing to answer it, Waffles nipping at my ankles.

"Peyton—" My words die on my lips.

I don't think I've ever seen her so gutted. Her eyes are red rimmed, and her cheeks are puffy.

"What happened?"

I hold open my arms, ready to wrap her in them, but she brushes by me.

Shit. This isn't good.

"Earl fired me."

"What happened?" Based on the lack of news surrounding me right now, I'm guessing I know. But I need her to confirm it.

"He found out about us."

"How?" Tension builds in my neck, and I rub a hand over it, trying to work out the knots.

"I don't know!" Peyton explodes, tears spilling down her cheeks. "Everything was going fine. No one knew about us, and now I have no job!"

It's Peyton's turn to pace. Waffles is sitting on the couch, his head bouncing between both of us like a tennis match.

"What can I do to help?"

"How can you help? Earl has his rules!"

"Maybe I could change agents?"

"Get real," Peyton scoffs.

"I'm trying to come up with something to help."

"You have a contract with him. You can't just leave."

"Then what do you suggest?" My voice has more anger than I want, but the woman in front of me is frustrated. And angry and sad. It's a deadly combination.

"There's only a few weeks left in the semester. I doubt I'll be able to get credit hours for anything I've done this semester. And I can't graduate without them."

This time, when I walk over to Peyton, she lets me wrap her up in my arms. "We can figure this out together."

Peyton doesn't say anything, but just buries her face into my chest. It has my anxiety rising.

"I know it doesn't seem like it right now, but we'll get through this." I run my hands through her hair, trying to calm her down.

"The reason I'm in this mess in the first place is because we're together."

"What are you saying?"

Fear blankets me. Sure, I knew Peyton had her doubts about the two of us. I just never thought I'd see it so clearly on her face. Peyton pushes off of me, crossing her arms in front of her.

"I just need some time to figure this out," she whispers.

"Peyton, time won't help." I go to reach for her again, but she dodges my hand. I can feel her slipping away.

"Colin." When she looks at me, my heart breaks.

It fucking cracks in my chest. Tiny shards are falling at my feet with each tear that slips down her cheeks.

"Don't do this, Peyton." I shake my head. I don't want to lose her. I *can't* lose her again.

Losing her once changed everything.

Losing her again?

I don't think I'd ever be able to recover from it.

"I'm beginning to think it might've been easier if we'd just left our past in the past."

"We can figure this out. I can find you another agent to work for."

Peyton walks up to me, pressing a hand into my chest.

I clutch it to me. Because I know, I just fucking know, it's going to be the last time. That when she walks out that door, I won't see her again.

The woman who crushed me in college is breaking me again.

"Goodbye, Colin."

I can't force the words out.

They're too real. Too final.

I can't look at her, but I drink her in one last time. Even with tears streaming down her face, she's the most beautiful woman I've ever known.

The only woman I've ever loved. No one knows me better than Peyton. I've never wanted anyone to see me the way she does. She is the only one worthy.

And now, she's leaving. She's giving Waffles one last scratch on the head and turning away from me.

I wait. And I watch.

I want her to realize that everything she just said was a big mistake and that we'll figure this out together. But I see her breathe in and open the door.

Just like that, she's gone.

And whatever is left of my heart turns to ash.

Because fuck.

Peyton is really gone.

Chapter Thirty

PEYTON

"How long are you going to stay in bed?" Grier curls up beside me.

"About as long as it takes for me to get over Colin." His name on my lips has my heart clutching in my chest.

"Sweetheart. There has to be something out there for you." Grier brushes my hair off my forehead.

"I've looked. There are no other agencies based in Denver."

"What about the one Colin used to have as representation?"

I shake my head into my pillow. "They moved out to Vegas when the team settled there. There's no one."

"Damn."

"I should've known better." I squeeze my eyes shut, trying to stop another onslaught of tears. With no job to go to, I've had little to distract myself from the pain in my heart.

"You couldn't have known this would happen."

"Earl told me on the first day about the no-fraternization policy. I broke that rule."

"But how did he find out?"

That's the million-dollar question. Colin and I were careful at every event. We never touched, never hugged. I made sure we were professional.

So what slipped through the cracks?

"I don't know. But does it even matter anymore?"

I bury my face into the pillows, hiccupping through another round of tears.

Will these ever stop?

"Okay. I cannot take seeing you like this. It's breaking my own heart. We need to do something that will help."

"I don't want to go drinking."

"Psh." Grier slaps me on the arm. "I have something else in mind."

AN HOUR LATER, Grier is dragging me into a boxing studio.

"You know I've never done this, right?"

She nods. "Yes, but you need a better release than crying in your room at all hours of the day."

"You can hear me?"

"The walls are paper-thin. Of course I can hear you."

"Sorry."

Wrapping an arm around my shoulders, Grier tugs me into her side. "It's okay. I don't know what you're feeling, but I hate that you're going through this."

"I'm glad I have you."

"And you always will." Grier steers me toward a free-standing bag. "And now, you get to punch the shit out of something."

I grab the pair of gloves she's holding in front of me. "So what, I just start hitting?"

"Yup." She pops the p. "I've been here a few times, and it's free bag time, so you just start hitting."

"You know I'm going to be terrible at this?"

"Nah. I've seen you put your mind to things, Peyton. You'll figure it out."

Grier moves to stand behind the bag as I wrap the gloves around my wrists. They're bulky and oversized, but big enough to protect my hands.

I shake out my arms before striking the bag. I bounce off it easily, making no impact.

"Hand up by your chin. Set your feet before you strike so you get more force behind your hit," Grier instructs.

This time, I make contact with the center of the bag. "Fuck, that felt amazing."

"Right?" Grier's eyes are glowing. "Just keep doing that."

I don't wait for her to finish, striking the bag a second time.

"How did I not know you come and do this all the time?"

Grier shrugs a shoulder. "It's my self-care time. Helps me clear my head."

I hook my arm into the bag. Again and again.

I don't stop. I just keep smacking the bag as hard as I can.

For the first time in a week, my head feels clear. The fuzziness that has been living there dissipates. It felt like I was moving in quicksand and couldn't catch my breath.

With each strike on the bag, I feel somewhat better.

The kind of love Colin and I had burned hot and bright. The pain of losing him won't go away anytime soon. But I know I'll have Grier by my side every step of the way.

"Damn, girl. You should do this more often."

I shake out my arm, feeling the burn. "It feels good."

"You look better." Grier clutches the bag, smiling at me.

Resting my gloved fists on my hips, I heave in a deep breath. "Maybe I should just do this every day, and I'll eventually get over him."

"You'll be ready to be an MMA fighter if you keep that up."

"Maybe that can be my new career path." Reality hits me.

When I wake up tomorrow, I won't have a job to go to.

I won't have Colin.

I'll be lucky if I find a way to finish my degree.

I love this place. It's become my second home after leaving Knoxville. I never wanted to leave. But maybe I can find my dream position in a different city.

Even though it won't have Colin.

That's a dream that I have to give up.

Because the two of us just weren't meant to be.

Damn it. Why did I have to let my heart rule everything? What a fickle bitch.

Chapter Thirty-One

COLIN

"You're pushing too hard," Alex pipes up as I press the weight bar up again.

The burn is the only thing distracting me from the pain in my chest. This time, there wasn't any doubt that Peyton walked away from me.

From us.

"I'm fine," I growl.

"Stop." Alex grabs the bar, not letting me finish my set. "You're going to hurt yourself, and then who will I have out on the field with me?"

"I can think of about fifty-one other players."

"Don't be a shithead."

"Wouldn't be anything new," I grumble.

When I go to walk away, Alex pulls me back. "Colin. What's wrong?"

My skin feels too tight, like at any moment I'm going to burst into tiny pieces because she's not here with me.

"Peyton left."

"What? When did you two start dating?"

I love Alex, but during the season, his sole focus is football, and most things tend to pass by him.

"For the last couple of weeks."

Sixty-seven days to be exact.

Not that anyone is counting.

"Shit. How did I miss that?"

"Well, you didn't miss anything. We weren't supposed to be together, and now we're not. End of story."

Alex shakes his head, taking a swig of water. "Doesn't sound like end of story to me."

"She lost her job because we were together."

"And that's it? Just like that?"

"Just like that."

"Huh." Alex stalks away from me.

"Huh what?"

Fucker. Dropping a cryptic bomb like that and walking away.

"Never thought you were a quitter," he throws over his shoulder.

Before I can get to him, Coach walks into the room. "James. A word."

My shoulders curl in as I follow him out of the weight room and toward his office. I've been in a shitty mood this week, and it's shown. Dropped passes. Missed routes. It's like I'd never played a down of football in my life.

"You wanted to see me?" Shutting the door behind me, I sit in front of his desk. He has more pictures of his family than football decorating his office.

"You've been off this last week. What's going on?"

"Did Alex talk to you?" Now I really wanted to give it to him.

"No. It's obvious to anyone that you're hurting because your game is off. And believe it or not, I pay attention. What happened?"

He stares at me. His salt-and-pepper hair and brown eyes give him a kind appearance. One that makes him easy to talk to. That has me spilling my guts.

It's cathartic getting it all out.

"I don't know what else I can do. I can't lose her." The confession slips out. I stare at my fidgeting hands.

I've lost Peyton once. I can't lose her again. Even these few days without her have been too much.

"I had a call with Earl today."

My head pops up. "Why did my agent call you?"

Sure, Earl and Coach were friendly. But it's not like they had to work together frequently.

"To discuss your situation."

It feels like the small room is closing in on me. "My situation?"

Please don't tell me I was called in here to be cut.

"Earl had high praise for you. Said you've done a great job of turning things around. We all see it. You're an asset to this organization and we're lucky to have you. You won't be going anywhere."

"Thank fuck." I can't hide my relief. "Talk about a rollercoaster of emotions."

Coach laughs. "Sorry, Colin. I don't mean to stress you out. But I did talk to the GM."

"This is you not stressing me out?" I blow out a breath.

"Suzanne is looking to take a step back and pass on some of her duties to someone else. With that, we'll need more help in our social media department—perhaps an intern. Think you know anyone who might want the job?"

"You're shitting me."

Coach laughs at me. "I promise you."

Pulling out a legal-size envelope, he hands it over to me. "I figured you might want to deliver the news in person. Suzanne has already contacted the university to work out any remaining credits."

"Holy shit."

Coach stands, walking around his desk. "Colin, I'm always here for you guys. If you're hurting, I want to make it better. Get your head on straight. Go get your girl back, and we'll see you before the game."

He doesn't have to tell me twice.

I'm up and out of his office.

Because the only thing I want to do now is get Peyton back.

In my arms where she belongs.

Chapter Thirty-Two

PEYTON

A knock at the door has me pulling my heavy body off the couch. For the last few days, I've been going to Grier's gym to beat the shit out of the heavy bags.

It's my version of therapy.

Except my entire body feels like a noodle.

But when I swing the door open, it's not the delivery guy.

It's Colin.

"What are you doing here?"

"Hoping to give you everything you want in life."

He looks just as tired as I do.

I sigh. "Colin—"

"Look, before you say anything, let me just say this, okay?"

I nod.

"You like stats, so let me give you some stats on our relationship."

Sucking in a deep breath, I steady myself on the door.

"I've been in love with you for seven years. Since the

moment I laid eyes on you. Every second of every minute of every hour of every day. For seven damn years."

He takes a step closer.

"I've loved you across every mile that was between Denver and Knoxville. All fourteen hundred of them."

Another step closer.

"We had Mexican seventy-two nights in college. Because two college kids on a budget loved free taco night."

"Oh God. I forgot how many tacos we ate those nights," I groan.

Colin smiles and takes a step closer to me.

"I know how many days we were apart those two years —about fifty-six. Because every time there was an away game, I hated leaving you. But I loved studying with you. A kiss for every right answer, remember?"

We both smile at the memory.

"I remember the day I said I loved you for the first time. Do you remember?"

A small smile pulls at the corner of my mouth. The memory has my heart catching in my chest.

"It was after that crappy loss against Mississippi. It was pouring down rain and I tweaked my shoulder. You were the only one there for me at that game. I don't think I've ever felt more loved, except when you took care of me after my concussion."

"Someone had to take care of you."

Colin closes the distance between us, the front of his tennis shoes nearly connecting with my bare toes. "And I'm glad it was you. Something changed for me that day. I knew I'd never be happy unless you were in my life."

He takes my small hand in his much larger one. "My favorite thing was holding your hand. *Is* holding your hand. I always wanted to be connected to you. And without you, these last few years have been hard. No one could ever replace you, Peyton."

A tear slips out of his eye. It has the tears that have been gathering in my own eyes sliding down my face.

"I love you, Rocky. You're the best thing that's ever happened to me, and I don't know what I'd do if I lost you for good. Without a doubt, you're the best catch I've ever made."

A watery laugh escapes. "A little cheesy, don't you think?"

"What can I say? You bring it out in me, Rocky."

"It doesn't change the facts, Colin. I can't get a job in Denver."

"You sure about that?" He waves the folder he's been holding.

"What is that?"

"A job with the Mountain Lions."

"You're kidding."

He shakes his head. "Earl made some calls. The Communications Director is taking a step back so they'll need the help. Social media, press releases…all sorts of things. It's still an internship, but it'd be perfect for you."

Colin holds out the envelope and I tear it open. Written right there are the details of the job, starting in January with the new semester.

"Oh my God. You're serious."

"I want this to work, Peyton. I want you to stay here. To work for the team I play for. To be a family with me and Waffles."

I swipe the tears away. "How is Waffles?"

"He misses you. Just like I do."

He cups my cheeks. "What do you say, Peyton?"

Every single word he's said settles into the cracks of my

heart, stitching them back together. Wrapping my fist in his shirt, I pull him into me.

In an instant, a smile paints his handsome face as I say, "It's a good thing you won't mind working with me then. Because I guess I'm going to keep you around for a while."

His shoulders sag in relief, like he's finally released the weight of the world that he's been carrying. "God, I fucking love you, Peyton."

His lips attack mine in a bruising kiss. Everything we're feeling is poured into this kiss as we fight for control. I forgot how good he tastes. Even a little over a week apart was too long.

Lifting me into his arms, he backs us into my apartment, not breaking the kiss. Dropping the envelope, I feel his muscles flex under my fingertips as I cling to him. I never want to be apart from this man.

Colin kicks the door shut behind him, setting me down on the entry table. His lips drift down the soft column of my neck. My pulse is rapid under his touch.

"I need to be inside you."

I don't need any more encouragement. Quick fingers are working his pants open and shoving them down his legs. He's hard as a rock. I love how I can turn this man on.

Colin's face is centimeters from mine. I drag a finger over his lips, missing the feel of them. "I missed you."

He grabs my hand, pressing a kiss in my palm. "I was going fucking crazy without you."

"You still managed to play some pretty good football." I wiggle out of my shorts.

"Practice was terrible, but it was the only thing I could do to numb the pain."

"I love you," I whisper as Colin slides inside of me on a gasp.

"I love you, Peyton. It's you and me."

I hug him to me, feeling every bit of his bare, hard length as he's thrusting in and out of me. Words of love are whispered as we come together. Our breaths are coming fast as we stay connected, neither of us wanting to move.

"As long as you score three touchdowns," I say, smiling into his neck.

"For you, Peyton? I'll make it four."

Chapter Thirty-Three

This sucks. Another season, and we're out of the playoffs in the wildcard round. To add insult to injury, Vegas beat us.

Locker clean-out day is the worst. Every face in here is sad. The jubilant energy we had at the start of the season is nowhere to be found. But the new intern in the communications department—who also happens to be my favorite person in the world—arranged a team luncheon afterward.

So I can't be too upset.

The buzzing of my phone pulls me away from dumping old shampoo bottles out of my locker.

Dad.

As much as I want to ignore him, I don't. Because he won't stop until I answer.

"Dad."

"Colin. Pretty sloppy game you had yesterday. Losing to Vegas?" He tsks.

I really should have declined the call.

"It happens." I don't want to get into it with him.

"Maybe if you weren't screwing around with that

woman, your head would've been in the game where it was supposed to be."

"Are you fucking kidding me with this shit?" Dropping the towel in my hand, I walk out into the hallway to get more privacy.

"That's no way to talk to your father."

"Maybe when you act like my father, I'll talk to you the way you deserve," I snap.

"You were never like this when you weren't with that woman. I thought I got rid of her the first time. I can't believe you got back together with her."

My vision blurs as anger pulses through me. "What?"

"You needed to focus on football, so I did what I had to do."

Clarity hits me. "It was you who wrote the letters in college. You were the one who got her fired."

"You were—*are*—throwing your future away. Football should be your focus. Winning a Super Bowl." He states this like it's the most obvious fact in the world.

"You had no right to do that!" I shout. I don't need to know any more. He's the reason Peyton and I weren't together all those years. It has a fire-breathing dragon ready to burst out of me.

"I'm your father—"

"No." I cut him off. "You don't get to play that card. The only thing you cared about was my football stats. You couldn't hack it as a player, but if my stats weren't perfect, you couldn't give a shit."

"Watch your mouth."

"I'm done, Dad. If this is how you want to treat me, treat the woman *I'm fucking in love with*, then we're done. You only see me as a player. When you start treating me as your son, then we can talk."

I end the call, nearly crushing my phone in my fist.

Anger seethes through me. I have the confirmation that he kept Peyton and me apart. I still remember those early days after the draft, wanting to call Peyton and talk to her. Try to make her understand that we should be together.

But he was the one that talked me out of it. The one that kept us apart.

The need to see her trumps everything else right now. I don't care that my locker is half-empty.

I need Peyton.

My strides are fast as I head down the hall toward the management offices. I turn the corner and she's there.

The moment she spots me, her smile drops as she walks over to me. "What happened?"

"My dad."

Her lips turn up in a snarl. "What'd he do?"

"You were right." Clasping her hand in mine, I drag her out of the main part of the hallway. "He was the one that broke us up all those years ago. Did it again, in fact. No idea how he got to Earl, but I'm sure he has his ways."

"Colin. I'm so sorry." She doesn't rub in the fact that she guessed right. Even though my dad is a dick, I didn't want her to be right about this. "How're you holding up?"

I pull her into my arms, breathing in her jasmine perfume and vanilla body wash. It's an instant balm on my frayed nerves. "I just can't believe it."

"I wish it weren't true."

Her arms are the only thing keeping me grounded. I wish my dad wasn't like this. That he wasn't the world's biggest dick. But I guess when you're washed-up, you take it out on the person who made it. It doesn't matter right now. Because the only important person in my life is the woman in my arms.

"I'm just glad you're here, Rocky," I whisper, my voice catching.

"There's nowhere else I'd rather be. Well…"

"Well what?" I ask, popping back.

Her eyes are playful. "I do actually have to be at the team luncheon right now. Think you could walk over there with me?"

I blow out a breath, running my hand down her arm to take her hand in mine. "And show off my girl? Abso-fuckin-lutely."

Peyton's smile is bright as we walk through the building toward the indoor practice field. Long tables of food are set up around smaller tables for seating. Families are already waiting for the players.

Earl spots us from across the room and walks over to us. "Colin. Peyton. It's nice to see you two here together."

Peyton shakes his hand, and he claps me on the back.

"I guess I have you to thank for getting me this job."

He waves her off. "I know good talent when I see it. I knew the Mountain Lions would be a good fit for you. Are you sure you want to be with this guy though?" He thumbs at me.

Peyton looks me up and down, as if deciding. "Eh. I think I'll keep him."

"Ouch, Rocky. Ouch." I pull her into my arms, smothering her in my chest. Her shoulders are shaking with laugher.

Just a few weeks ago, I never thought this would be our future. But now, we're here together, out in the open. The playful way we love each other is on full display.

"At least I know you'll keep him in line." Earl shakes his head, walking over to see the GM who has now arrived.

"What's going on over here?" Alex appears behind us.

"Trying to keep Colin in line." Peyton spins in my arms but doesn't move.

Alex's eyes flit between the two of us. "So I finally get to *officially* meet the famous Peyton as your girlfriend?"

"The one and only." I squeeze her closer to me.

Alex wraps his arms around both of us in the most awkward of hugs. "Then let me say thank you for making this guy get his shit together. I didn't want to lose my wide receiver."

"Aww. You really do like me."

"What can I say? I didn't want to have to break in a new guy." Alex pushes back, smiling down at Peyton like they're the best of friends now.

"You tell me when he's acting up, and I'll take care of him," Peyton chides.

"Oh great, now you two are going to be ganging up on me?" I roll my eyes.

"Don't fight it. You know you love it." Peyton pinches my cheek.

Except I do. I really fucking do.

Because I get the best of both worlds.

Football and Peyton.

The day is finally here. My gown swishes around my ankles as I wait my turn. I don't know who decided to do this outside in May, but it's blisteringly hot today.

"Peyton Thompson."

I walk across the stage as my name is called to accept my diploma. I hear my name shouted from the other side of the stadium where my small group is cheering me on. Grier is right behind me.

"We did it!" She nearly tackles me in a hug as we take our seats to listen to the last of the graduates get called.

"We're done! Holy shit!" I breathe a sigh of relief.

I didn't think this day would ever come. When I lost my internship with Earl, I had no idea what would happen. I was able to work it out to get the credits I needed to graduate this spring, but it wasn't easy. I was doing the jobs of two people most days.

I should've known better. Colin was there for me when I needed him the most. Even though it hasn't been easy, these past few months have been some of the best of my life.

Every day, I get to go to work for the best organization in the league. And at night? I get to go home to my two favorite guys.

Waffles is obviously first. Colin is a very close second.

With my internship now over, the thought of looking for a job is daunting. But that's a problem for Monday.

Right now, I'm ready to toss this cap and celebrate with my friends and family.

And sleep.

That final thesis took nearly everything out of me. Thank God it's the off-season, or I don't know what I'd have done.

As the final person walks across the stage, Grier and I link arms. She's already accepted a job out west for a minor league baseball team that's been in hot water. She said she's ready for the challenge…and guys in baseball pants.

"Congratulations, graduates," the chancellor announces as caps are thrown high into the air. I bring Grier into a rib-crushing hug. Tears are threatening to spill over. My emotions have been on a hair trigger all day. As much as I'm looking forward to the next chapter in my life, I hate that Grier and I won't see each other every day.

Families make their way onto the field, and Grier rushes off to find hers. Arms wrap around me from behind, swinging me back and forth.

"I am so fucking proud of you!" My head hits Colin's shoulder as happiness bursts out of me.

"I can't believe I'm done!" He sets me down, and I spin to pull him tight to me.

"Finally time for fucking vacation!"

Colin told me he wanted to go on vacation after the postseason loss. But with school, I couldn't get the time off.

Now, the only thing that stands between Colin and me and the beach are just a few short days.

"Mmm. I'm ready for a few cocktails by the beach. Think I could find a cabana boy to bring them to me?"

"God, can you two get a room?" Alex walks up behind Colin.

"Sorry, man." Colin shrugs, but he's not actually sorry.

"Congratulations, Peyton." Alex leans down, giving me an awkward side hug since Colin's arms are still around me.

"Thanks. I'm so happy you could come today."

Alex and I have gotten close since I started working with the team. He's one of the nicest guys, and I love how close he and Colin are.

"Well, I also come bearing some good news." He pulls a crinkled envelope out of his jacket pocket.

"What's this?" I take the envelope from him and tear it open.

"Team thought it would be fun to deliver this today."

Colin moves to stand beside Alex. Both of them are crossing their arms, looking down at me.

If I didn't know any better, I'd say they were brothers.

The Mountain Lions logo is at the top of the paper.

The contents?

A full-time position as the teams new social media coordinator.

My jaw drops as my eyes ping-pong between the two guys standing in front of me.

"This isn't a joke, right?" My eyes get watery looking at the letter given to me.

"Do you really think I'd pull something like that?" Alex says.

"This is real? The Mountain Lions want me?"

"Fuck yeah they do!" Colin shouts.

"Oh my God!" I leap into Colin's arms, crushing the offer letter in my hand. Alex laughs at the two of us.

"I take it that means you're accepting the job?" Alex asks.

"This is only my dream job!" I wrap an arm around Alex and pull him into my hug. "I can't believe this is happening!"

"Believe it, Peyton. You deserve it." Alex steps back. "I'll meet you in the parking lot."

Alex leaves Colin and me together. Grasping his face, I attack his face with kisses.

"I can't believe I get to keep my job!"

"The team would be crazy to let you go."

Tears start to run down my face at everything that is happening. Everything that I've ever wanted is finally mine.

Dream guy and dream job. Even if it took us a few years to get here, I wouldn't change a thing.

Colin and football.

It doesn't get any better than that.

THE END

Bonus Scene

PEYTON

"Okay, stay right there. Good boy." Colin backs slowly away from Waffles as he turns his head to look at me.

He's making the same face I am - *is this guy for real?*

"Okay, Rocky, grab the picture."

"You're ridiculous," I laugh as I snap a few pictures of Waffles in a Santa costume in front of the Christmas tree.

"You mean amazing. People are going to love this. Hopefully it'll help get more dogs adopted before the holidays."

If I wasn't a puddle of goo before, I am now.

Who would've thought the biggest playboy in the league would have the softest heart?

I knew, because this is the Colin that I've always known. Who puts everyone else before him. He just went into hiding for a few years.

"Why do you have that dopey grin on your face?" Colin hefts the growing dog into his arms, smothering him in kisses.

"Just thinking how great you are." I walk over and plant an obnoxiously loud kiss on his lips.

"You might be thinking for a while."

"I've got some time." I snuggle deeper into Colin's arms. The fire is crackling as it gets darker outside. About a foot of snow was dumped on Denver last night, making it the perfect day for an early Christmas celebration.

With the holiday on a Sunday, the team will be gone for the weekend. Practice was canceled on Friday so everyone could enjoy the day with their families.

And with my parents visiting my brother, Colin and I chose to stay here together.

"I'm glad you're here," Colin whispers, dipping down to take my lips in a sweet kiss. It's like he can read my mind.

"There's nowhere else I'd rather be."

"Good." A playful smile slides across his face. "Because it's time to take Waffles out to play in the snow."

"Just because you love the snow, doesn't mean he will."

"I got him a little vest and booties. He has to like the snow!"

I laugh as we throw on our heavy coats and Colin changes Waffles from his Santa costume to cold weather gear.

"Okay, let's go bud." Colin opens the sliding glass door from the kitchen into the backyard. Waffles looks at him like he's crazy.

"Why isn't he going?" Colin looks at me with a confused expression.

"Probably because he doesn't want to wear all this stuff." I roll my eyes at him before taking off the booties. "Just let him run around. He'll love it."

As soon as the booties are off, he takes off into the snow, jumping into the snow.

"Why'd that work?" Colin huffs, crossing his arms.

"You're overthinking it. Just let him play and get used to the snow." I wrap my arms around him, watching the energetic pup.

Fat snowflakes are falling from the sky. The lights from the tree cast a magical glow through the windows.

And with my arms wrapped around Colin, it feels pretty damn perfect.

"You know, I feel like we need to commemorate our first holiday together."

"Oh yeah? What are you thinking?" Colin takes a step back into the snow. I don't like the gleam in his eyes.

"How about an annual snowball fight?" He lobs a handful of snow my way. The cold trickles through my coat and down my back.

"Oh, it is so on!" With less grace than I normally possess, I start throwing snow Colin's way.

"You're going to have to do better than that!" Colin ducks behind the table, now buried beneath the snow.

"Not all of us are NFL quarterbacks," I laugh, chucking another snowball in his direction.

"I'm not either, and I still have better aim than you!" This time, Colin nails me square in the chest.

"You better watch the goods."

"Oh, I'm sorry. Did I hurt you?" Colin steps around the table, his hands raised in surrender.

"I just don't want–" but Colin tackles me before I can say anything. We land with a soft *oomph* in the snow.

"You are such a dirty player." But my words hold no heat. I'm laughing as Waffles jumps into the pile.

"Attack, Waffles, attack!" I shout as Colin starts to tickle me. Waffles only licks the snow off my face, his nose cold. "Not me!"

I try to push him off, but he only nuzzles deeper into

my neck. Colin flops back into the snow, holding his stomach in laughter.

"He loves me too much to attack me. Good boy, Waffles."

"We need more female energy in this house." I sit up, scooping Waffles into my lap.

"Nah, I think we're good."

Snowflakes cling to Colin's lashes as he lays in the snow. His eyes are bright as they stare back at me.

"Just you wait, Colin James. I'm going to get Waffles here a sister."

"Are we going to become *that* family, Peyton? The one with eighty dogs running around?"

I shrug a shoulder. "I wouldn't mind it. If they're all as good as this little guy," I give Waffles an affectionate rub on the head, "then that's okay."

Colin sits up, brushing the hair back from my face. "If I get to have eighty dogs, I want them all with you."

My heart is overflowing with love for this man as I take his face in my hands and lay one on him. His lips are cold like mine, but what I feel for this man is anything but. I want to bottle this feeling and never let go of it.

"I love you," I whisper against his lips.

"I love you, Peyton." A yelp sounds next to us. Waffles is wagging his tail, snow clinging to his fur. "I love you too, Waffles."

"C'mon. Let's go get some hot chocolate and open presents."

Twenty minutes later, we're snuggled together in front of the crackling fireplace, two gift boxes in hand.

"Okay, you go first." He presses the small box with an overwhelming bow into my hands.

Finding the tape on the bottom, I unwrap the package to find a velvet box. "We said nothing expensive."

"Just open it." Colin pulls me closer to him as I open the box with a snap.

A gold football locket rests on the pillow. Pulling it out, I snap open the clasp and gasp. It's a picture of our first date on one side and another of us from the Mountain Lions game a few weeks ago. I'm in his arms, his name and number splashed across my back.

"Oh Colin." Tears wet my eyes as I wrap him in a hug. "It's beautiful."

"I know there's a lot of years missing in between, but as long as we can keep adding to it, well, that's all I want."

"Well now my gift seems dumb." I try to pull it away, but Colin grabs for it. Damn his good hands.

He opens the small envelope. His eyes trace over each of the words.

"You did your own relationship stats?"

I nod, twisting my hands in my lap. "I did. I figured I could show you just how much you mean to me."

"I don't know what I did to deserve you, Peyton."

"I'm just happy that it was you who walked into Earl's office that day. I can't imagine my life without you."

Colin drops his forehead to mine. "All I need is you."

"And you have me."

Forever.

Acknowledgments

Book 9 is out in the world!

With each book I'm writing in the Mountain Lions series, I'm falling more and more in love with these guys and this entire world! Football is family, and I love my new family that I've created!

I had so much fun creating Colin and Peyton and watching Colin redeem himself. He's a total softie for Peyton and it's those guys that I absolutely love! So I hope you fell in love with them like I did.

There are so many people to thank, and I always worry that I'm going to miss someone…

To each and every author friend, Norma, LJ, Swati, Claire, Suzanne, Alexandra…I can't thank you enough for your endless support! Without you, I wouldn't be where I am today!

To my Street Team…thank you for your loving on my books as much as I do!

To all the readers, bloggers, bookstagrammers, and booktokers…thank you for reading and taking a chance on my books! I couldn't do it without you.

<3 Emily

About the Author

After winning a Young Author's Award in second grade, Emily Silver was destined to be a writer. She loves writing strong heroines and the swoony men who fall for them.

A lover of all things romance, Emily started writing books set in her favorite places around the world. As an avid traveler, she's been to all seven continents and sailed around the globe.

When she's not writing, Emily can be found sipping cocktails on her porch, reading all the romance she can get her hands on and planning her next big adventure!

Find her on social media to stay up to date on all her adventures and upcoming releases!

The Love Abroad Series

An Icy Infatuation

A French Fling

A Sydney Surprise

Get all my titles now: